The Nocturnals

The Nocturnals

Aleksandra Rychlicka

The Nocturnals

Text copyright©2021 Aleksandra Rychlicka
Cover Design©2021 Jonathan C. Mientus

ISBN 978-1-8380247-2-7

First Published in Great Britain
1 3 5 4 2

Conditions of Sale

British Library Cataloguing in Publication Data.
A catalogue record for this book is available from the British Library.

Printed and bound in Great Britain by
CPI Group (UK) Ltd. Croydon CR0 4YY

Hawkwood Books 2021

To all the strangers out there, making their ways
in foreign lands and foreign languages.

NIGHT

MARO

The loud dance music pouring through Maro's headphones makes the world look like a video clip.

Tonight more than ever. Without the music he would be at a party. His party, strictly speaking, as the people he watches drinking and dancing are in his house. And the only thing Maro loathes more than being at a party is hosting one.

The music once again comes to his rescue, transforming the scene into a performance. Maro need not bother with the crowd. They're not his quests but tonight's artists; entertainers. It is him who is their audience.

Maro watches the people with an ease uncommon to him, recognising few of them and caring for none. He's certain he wouldn't have let them in his home. And yet he must admit that they fit this place perfectly. They're strangers here, and the Estate is a haven to strangers. A person must remain a foreigner to the place he lives in if he desires never to move on. That's what the Estate is for; a time loop.

The people gathered in his house tonight are from the outside. Oblivious to the rules that govern the Estate, they believe they're here to celebrate the five-year anniversary of Maro and the building. It's a trick, a story he told. The truth is that he wanted the world which he abandoned to pay him a visit, if only for one night.

His gaze moves from one person to the next, looking over to the open kitchen, which now serves as a bar. The sparse interior is furnished with bottles and people, who waste no time emptying them. It's the first time Maro remembers seeing so much life here. He likes it, even if it doesn't feel right. All this bustle and excitement mocks the Estate's seclusion. The performance he commissioned, and now enjoys watching, violates the premise of the place, in which he is nothing more than a guest. Maro knows it cannot go unnoticed, that he will be asked to pay. Something is about to happen. But maybe there is a part of him that likes that, too.

Maro's eyes brush across a woman struggling to open a bottle of champagne. He moves over to her friend, standing right beside her, pauses for a second, and then returns to the woman with the champagne.

Maro is not sure what exactly has caught his eye. He again looks to her friend, and then few other people standing around. He needs a point of reference to make a comparison. When he returns to the woman he knows what it is; the music fails to separate them. Looking at her Maro's right in, whether he likes it or not.

But before he can examine her more closely, the cork blasts out of the bottle. Just like the champagne, she, too, bursts into laughter, trying to quickly sip off the overflowing bubbles. And her laughter travels across the room, penetrating Maro's headphones, defeating the music. It's not possible, and yet Maro could swear he heard her.

Then something else grabs her attention. Something inside her purse. She tries to shake the champagne off her hands before reaching inside her bag. A phone, of course. He could've guessed.

She answers, covering her other ear, struggling to hear the caller. Maro doesn't need to hear to know it's bad news. The woman's face stiffens. It's either death or an accident, he thinks. Only these produce the terror which now paralyses her face.

The bad news travels fast, spreading over the rest of her body, and she loses control of her hands. The phone drops to the floor, followed by the champagne bottle, which shatters.

Luckily her legs don't seize up, letting her flee from the room. It's a healthy instinct; run.

As her friends follow her out of the room, Maro walks over to the spot where they were standing. He picks up the

4

phone from the puddle of champagne, and gives it a gentle pat. Don't shoot the messenger.

Maro's tenderness provokes an immediate reaction. The phone in his hand vibrates and rings, despite its encounter with the champagne.

He takes off his headphones. Straight away, Maro gets pushed out of the time loop and thrown right into the present, which is now ringing in his hand. The trance-like soundtrack of his life in the Estate is at once superseded, and labelled as the past. But Maro hasn't been in the present for years. His reactions are slow, rusty; he lacks the appropriate tools to respond. He knows he cannot answer the phone. But neither can he put the headphones back on.

Then he hears something else, as if a distant cry. It's too far away for Maro to hear the noise itself; what reaches him instead is an echo of the noise.

He turns his head in the direction of the weeping, relieved to have escaped the pressure of making the decision. But even if he picked neither the past nor the present, he's still made a choice. He has forged ahead, into the unknown.

The bathroom door slams open. The woman bursts out, barging through the shocked group of people and running ahead. Straight into Maro. The volume of her lament increases, exploding in Maro's face. But it bounces off him, moving away rapidly. He reaches out to her, wants to pull her back. Then he remembers he cannot; there is a ringing phone in his hand.

The woman sees and hears nothing. Maro watches her run towards the front door.

Unable to stop her, Maro decides to follow. He must catch her before she exits the building. The phone in his hand continues ringing. Ringing and vibrating, as if to make sure Maro doesn't forget it.

Just as he steps out of his apartment, the woman reaches the door at the far end of the corridor, which opens from the other side at exactly the same moment.

Christ, watch out! shouts Adam. The echo of his voice makes Maro's skin crawl.

I'm sorry, I'm so, so sorry! wails the woman. But crashing into Adam is not the reason why she is apologising.

The phone rings again.

You alright? What happened? Adam asks, looking behind the woman's shoulder to see where she is running from.

His gaze meets Maro's and they lock eyes. It takes a second or two, then Maro nods reluctantly. Fine, Maro's eyes say, fine then.

The phone rings. Or rather it gives one last ring before dying. There goes his present. So Maro, too, lets go. The phone smashes onto the floor.

But there are still the headphones. Maro puts them back on; the music explodes in his head once again. The world is nothing but a videoclip.

LIV

She cannot tell how long she has been running across the corridor. But she knows it's been long enough to get her out of the building, or even behind the gate. And yet she's still inside, as if unable to reach the entrance. She's not sure whether it is her who's not moving, or it is the corridor that keeps expanding. She doesn't care either way, all she wants is to already be on her way back. But back where?

There is no going back, she realises. In that very moment the inability to get out of the building no longer feels like a trap, but a rescue.

Her legs halt, her body relaxes. For a second she closes her eyes, breathing in deeply. When she reopens them, she finds herself at the end of the corridor, by the entrance door. Face to face with a man.

The man is talking to her, asking questions. But she

neither hears nor sees him. She notes his presence, but is too agitated to pay attention. It rarely happens to her; such unknowing exposure. She's used to being the one who looks first, and only then decides whether to be seen.

But it's too late now. She must take what's left, review the damage. How much of her could he see?

Liv jumps in her mind back to the party. Rewinding the footage, she realises her face must be covered in tears. And ink.

The tears are fresh. A few drops are still running down her face, even though she has stopped crying.

The ink is from a few minutes ago, when she bit her finger hard, trying not to scream.

Liv screamed of horror, seeing that the ink wouldn't come off, no matter how long she held her hands under a tap. Or how hard she was rubbing at it. Like she was trying to scratch it from her body. She thought she could wash off ink stains the way she saw people washing off blood. But it would not come out.

Tears and ink, that's all he must've seen. Enough to distract him, or anyone else, from looking for more. Liv feels a sense of relief. She's well equipped to cope with stories.

She looks up, at last ready to see him   .

Where are you going? the man asks. Liv freezes.

The man studies her for a moment. Liv lets him do this. She now had the time to prepare; clean the surfaces, hide the dirty laundry. She's ready for him to look.

He doesn't know. He smiles like an explorer, unaware that all he's getting to see are the usual tourist attractions. Liv smiles back with the satisfaction of seeing the same old trick still working.

Move in with me, he says.

Now it's her turn to study his face. Let him be very pure or very sinister, Liv prays. If he is pure, I won't be able to hurt him. He will wake up from me like from a bad dream, and all the harm won't amount to more than an insect bite. And if he is sinister, the harm has already been done and nothing I do can change it.

She can't tell now. She only knows how little of her he can see. That's a good thing. She doesn't want to be seen. Not after what just happened. To stay here with him would be to disappear. It is a miracle she wouldn't have dared ask for.

She nods.

The man puts the edge of his sleeve in his mouth and wets it. He uses it to remove the ink from Liv's mouth.

And what do I call you?

What would you like to call me?

His eyes shine with an unexpected thrill. So strong it blinds Liv, who steps back, suddenly uncertain about her stay here. But stepping back only takes her further inside the building. Inside his home.

The man moves forward, toward her. The door behind him close. He reaches out his hand and places it on the top of Liv's head. Slowly, he runs his fingers across her forehead, his fingertip across her eyebrow. He feels her cheekbones, her nasal bridge, the curve of her upper lip. As if she were at a facial fitting for a part she's about to start playing.

Helen, he says. I'd like to call you Helen.

FIRST DAYS

LIV

Where do you go, when you are neither asleep nor awake? What is this place that makes you both restless and numb?

Liv lacks a word to describe it, but she begins to suspect it might be where she belongs now. She takes an old word 'home', which has lost its meaning, and stitches it together with this new place, in which she has found herself. Sleeplessness might be an exile, but she is determined to make herself at home here.

The midday sun enters the room. Liv squints her eyes. She wishes she could have just closed the curtains, pull down the shatters. But the windows here, just like the walls, are bare. The glass in them is electrochromic; it changes from clear to opaque depending on the sunlight. Smart technology, Adam explained with pride. He listed the many advantages: cutting-edge, energy-saving, protective of the environment.

It's also self-regulating. There is no remote control, no button to press. The windows decide when you are to sit in the darkness and when to blind you with sunlight.

Liv wouldn't call them smart exactly; intelligent, yes. Definitely vicious. At first she thought there's an error and the glass keeps changing from transparent to tinted at random. Now she begins to see the pattern. The windows use sunlight to make staying inside the house during the day as uncomfortable as possible.

Adam wouldn't know. He leaves the house when it's still dark and returns when it's dark again. The darkness outside is a prerequisite to use electric lights; they're disabled during the daytime.

Liv sits up, looking around in confusion.

Just as she regains focus, she spots a couple of pens on the table. Strange, there are rarely any objects lying around Adam's house. Everything needs to be hidden, cleared. Why then now, a pair of pens? Like they were left here on purpose. To tease her; to offend.

Liv picks the pens up, as carefully as if she was touching dangerous objects. She weighs the pens in one hand. She caresses them, tenderly sliding her fingers across.

She closes her fist and waits. Each morning finds her a little weaker. She is unsure whether she can still bring her body to carry out her orders. Then she remembers that night. The sound of her phone ringing, the voice on the other side. She breaks the pens in one violent gesture.

Liv opens her palms and watches the broken pens fall on the floor. She looks at her hands. A few sharp pieces of plastic pierce her skin. She buries her hands in her blazer. Adam's blazer.

She feels she can't breathe here anymore. The sunlight intensifies, turning the flat into a greenhouse. She must get out of this apartment.

Before she goes, there is something else she needs to do.

She runs outside.

She stands in front of the lift for five hundred seconds. Maybe longer, her count is slow. If so, it might even come up to ten minutes. The lift seems frozen.

She is on the seventh floor. There must be an emergency staircase. She looks around, spots one.

Walking down the stairs feels less like escaping and more like falling.

The moment Liv enters the hallway, the lift opens. Inside the lift there is a couple, kissing intimately. They are dressed alike, all in black.

Liv watches the couple like a film on the screen. They feel unreal. And so does she.

Only when the woman suddenly winks at her, Liv lowers her gaze. She points to the lift.

I'm sorry... but did you notice any problems with the lift? Didn't work when I tried calling... she explains.

Works just fine, the woman says.

Did you take the stairs? the man asks.

Liv nods.

Which floor? he asks.

Seventh, Liv answers.

The man pauses for a moment, considering something.

Seventh? But that's Adam and...

Helen, the woman interjects.

I'm Helen, Liv says. She is surprised how right those words sound, how well they make her feel. She turns around without waiting for their reactions.

She paces to the entrance and tries to push it open. The door won't budge.

The couple slowly walks up to the door. She can hear them halting behind her back. She pushes the door again, several times, shifting her whole weight. The door does not move an inch.

The man reaches out for the handle and pulls it with ease.

Not your day? the woman asks.

I just thought it's 'push', not 'pull', Liv laughs.

It isn't, the woman says with a stern expression.

No, I guess not, Liv responds, looking away.

The couple are about to pass Liv but the man turns around, pointing to her hands.

What happened? he asks.

It's nothing, she says, closing her stained and scratched fists.

The man and the woman exchange glances. Liv feels pressured to explain herself.

I guess I've been a little clumsy lately. New place, you know. Takes some time to adjust, she retreats to the line Adam has been serving her daily.

The man slowly runs his gaze across Liv's face. She knows he sees exactly what she has been seeing every morning. A pair of violet, puffy plums, growing under her eyes.

You seem to have adjusted very well, he says.

MARO

During the day the music sounds softer. It's an illusion; Maro keeps it on full volume at all times. But maybe there is a correlation between light and sound. Maybe the night carries less distractions and the tunes feel enough then. Maybe the day requires more effort to stay awake.

Maro pops an ice cube in his mouth and lets it melt. His eyelids grow heavy. He needs all his strength to keep them open. He presses the headphones against his ears. Even the tiniest upturn in sound can make a difference.

He cannot afford to lose energy. It is crucial not to make a single unnecessary move. He sits still, staring into space. Then something appears in his vision. A silhouette. His reflex is dulled. Only when the person vanishes from his sight, he realises it was the woman.

Hey! Maro shouts.

He manages to turn his head and sees that the woman has just reached the entrance. He can't tell whether she's heard him. After a second or two, she turns around. The woman looks in his direction, but it is unclear whether she sees him.

I know her, but she has never even seen me, Maro realises.

He forces himself to move. His body is weak, he cannot stand up. But he manages to raise his hand. I must look like a bench statue, Maro thinks.

The woman hesitates, then starts walking in Maro's direction. Only when closer, Maro notices she is holding a package. There is something unusual about the way she carries it, with almost straight arms. It allows her to keep the package as far away from herself as possible. As if she wants nothing to do with it.

Maro takes off the headphones but doesn't switch off the music. They hang around his neck, a security blanket in case his body fails him. The woman is now close enough to hear the music. Maro notices how her head automatically picks up on the rhythm, making tiny waves, backward and forward and backward; on repeat.

Maro uses the distance between them to size her up discreetly. She looks like someone who could use a change of soundtrack to her life.

I wanted to call your name then realised I don't know what to call you, Maro says with a smile when the woman approaches the bench.

She cannot help but smile back, even though last night might have left her convinced she would never do it again. But no amount of tragedy can crash a really great smile. Maro knows; he's always got one. And so does she.

It's Li... she begins.

Helen! The name, shouted from afar, superimposes itself on the woman's answer. Maro's skin crawls, an involuntarily reaction every time he hears Adam speak.

The woman doesn't yet recognise that sound. May she never know it the way I do, Maro thinks. The way Helen did.

She turns her head towards the noise and sees Adam, waving at them from afar. She quickly turns away. Her eyes meet Maro's. He is surprised with the scale of panic that takes over her face. She pushes her package onto Maro's lap.

Would you take it? She phrases the sentence as a question, but intonates it like a command. Not someone accustomed to having her will disobeyed.

But Maro is in no rush. He pops an ice cube in his mouth and plays with it.

Helen? You don't look like a Helen.

The woman shrugs her shoulders. It's not impatience; it's resignation. She barely looks at Maro, but assumes she sees everything there is to him. Barely listens, but believes she hears everything he says. And everything he silences. I have met many of you before, her face says, and I'm doomed to meet many more in the future.

Does it make a difference?

15

You tell me, Maro says, but knows she wouldn't tell him anything if it wasn't for the fear.

Maro looks sideways, measuring the time he's got. Adam's now less than a couple of minutes away.

Can you just take this away from me? Please? The woman is pleading now, trying to sound helpless. Maro wouldn't care much for that sudden change of voice, if there wasn't something in her that made him worried.

What is it? he asks, pointing at the package.

It's nothing, she snaps, then remembers he is not the fly she must keep away. She is.

The woman forces herself to smile. It gives Maro a chance to see what he must look like; dead eyes with a bright smile. I mean, it doesn't really matter, the woman explains. You're not to open it, she instructs him.

Maro realises she intended it to sound playful, but she failed to conceal the despair creeping in from behind the plea.

He moves his gaze from the woman to Adam who is now about a minute away. Maro can stall for time.

Tell me your name.

Maro's instinct is correct. The woman is desperate to get rid of the package.

It's Liv.

He knows she is telling the truth. To lie when you've only got one shot would be foolish. And she is no fool.

Liv pushes the package towards Maro.

Please? she says. Maro looks in her eyes and sees he was wrong. They're not quite dead. The worse for you, he thinks. Liv; life. Why then here, of all places? Buried alive.

Maro grabs the box at the very last moment and places it on his lap. Liv sighs with relief. But just as she wants to breathe in again, Adam reaches them and kisses Liv passionately.

He thinks he marks his territory.

16

Liv, taken aback, turns to Maro with a somewhat embarrassed smile. Adam follows Liv's gaze. He looks at Maro as if he only just saw him.

I see you've got a package! he says, for some reason intonating it like a joke.

You see right, confirms Maro, taking the time to look into Adam's face. It is exactly what he expected; the glow. She lets you rest, Maro realises, moving his gaze to Liv. He scans the damage in her face but is relieved to see that she knows. Or at least knows enough to realise that Adam's a predator, even if he looks like prey. But maybe that's what she is too, Maro now wonders, studying her face. What I had run away from is worse than what I have just run into, her eyes say.

What's inside? asks Adam, not out of curiosity, but to interrupt the silent exchange that he had just witnessed.

I'm not quite sure, Maro admits.

Well, why don't you open it to find out?

Maro feels Liv's gaze pressing against his skin. He dislikes pressure. He looks down at the box and runs his finger across the brown tape sealing its sides.

Maybe. I haven't decided yet.

LIV

The darkness in the living room frames the unshuttered window. It takes away the distractions, allows for focus. The glass surface turns into a screen. Tonight it shows Maro on the bench, smoking.

The lamp post by the bench illuminates him clearly. Even from the seventh floor Liv can see the crescents of Maro's face.

She rests her forehead on the window and begins watching. The cold of the glass runs through her body, giving her the shivers. She shakes them off; refocuses.

Studying Maro requires her full concentration. She feels

there is a piece of him that she's been missing. The piece that would allow her not only to see him, but to understand what she sees.

She's tempted to start with his face but decides to zoom out. To take in the view of him, let it sink in. She immediately feels his weight. It drops on her, making it hard to breathe.

Maro's heavy. But not like a stone. More like a bear. A sad, wounded bear. There's power to him that now lays dormant. But it's still there. Liv can sense it; smell it. It's the thing that draws others to him, even though they might not be able to name it. Then again, it wouldn't have mattered if they could. Liv sees it, but she still can't resist wanting to be close to Maro.

Is that who you are? Liv wonders. A wounded bear that hid from the world to heal? Or suffer in solitude? Whichever it is, this place is your cave, Liv guesses. Your fort. You're just like me, she says out loud.

Suddenly Maro looks up. It feels like their eyes meet. Liv's heart stops for a moment. She pulls back, terrified. But after a second she laughs at herself. She's on the seventh floor, in a pitch dark apartment. There isn't a way he could possibly know she's here.

She steps back to the window, looking at Maro's face looking at her. You can't see me, Liv forces herself to say. And so I won't turn away.

She goes back to studying him. Time to zoom in on his face. There is something odd about it. She noticed it the first time they met. The features are fine. Symmetrical. It could have been a beautiful face, had he only wanted it to be. It might have been once. Beauty is always a choice, and for now he can't be bothered. Nothing unusual here.

What puzzles Liv is a contradiction she reads in his face. Maro's at once resigned and wilful, apathetic and vigilant. He comes across as both inanimate and remarkably humane. The element Liv's missing is the glue that keeps the two opposites together. That makes him a whole.

The light in the room suddenly switches on. Liv jumps back but Maro has already been looking up. There is not a chance he didn't see her. He knows she'd been watching him.

Do you have any idea what happened to all the pens in this house?! Adam's voice, together with the switched-on light, feels like an attack. On Liv's privacy, her space. She turns to him with contempt. Like to a trespasser who sneaked into her home by night.

She knows it's a silly idea. This is his place and if anyone is to be called an intruder, it's her. But Liv cannot help feeling it's a mistake. Houses don't belong to their owners, they belong to those who inhabit them. Adam is never here. She is. It's her home then. Hers and Helen's.

I can't find a single one! Adam adds in an offended tone of voice. It makes Liv wince. She suspects there are few things that he doesn't take as a personal affront.

Why do you need a pen? she asks with incredulit y, more suited to the pursuits of quills than regular pens. The best defence is a good offence, and there are no pens left in this house. Liv knows.

I've got to do some work, Adam says. Defensively. The trick proved a triumph.

Can't you use your computer? Liv continues her attack. Many years ago, she signed up for boxing. The first rule she learned - other than to look forward - was the power of repetition. The rule that if a strategy works, you repeat it. Only idiots change something that works. Instead, you repeat it. And then again. And again. Repeat until you perfect it. Only then are you allowed to change. Try a different move.

Adam blushes and looks away. He's ashamed, Liv notices with panic. That changes the rules of the game. Feelings always do. They annul the game, actually. How soon now will she have to look for another place?

Liv glances to the door. Adam catches her gaze, and

blushes even harder. He can read her panic. But not what caused it. He thinks it was his shouting that scared me, Liv guesses.

I'm sorry, he says. It's nothing urgent. I can do it tomorrow.

Adam walks up to Liv and kisses her. It's pleasant. Adam's a good kisser. Someone must've once told him kissing really matters. He does well on all the really important things. Now, kissing Liv, whom he neither knows nor cares about, he pours out his heart. It's a sound heart. One that still loves Helen. Liv can tell.

It just seems a bit odd, Adam says, pulling back a little. I always have dozens of pen laying around.... And now I can't find a single one.

Liv pulls Adam back to her. She kisses him the way she imagines that Helen would. With joy and delight, but without the pretence of love. Always keeping him right in front of an open door, letting him look inside but not to step in. She can tell he recognises the dynamics, takes comfort in the familiarity of her approach.

As Adam kisses Helen, Liv opens her eyes and sees Maro. He's now standing in front of the bench, his eyes still fixed on the window. He watches them kissing. She lets him watch. But keeps her own eyes open. She wants to watch Maro watching her.

ADAM

The sound doesn't wake him up at first. It breaks into his dream, sure. But it fails to break it down.

Dreams are a powerful thing. They're capable of not only defeating the waking reality, but subjugating it to serve their own purpose. At first, the rain outside transforms into hail, banging on the roof and windows of Adam's cottage. He can't be sure the cottage is really his, but he keeps returning

20

here in most of his dreams; the happy ones at least. Then again, ever since he started sleeping again, every dream is a happy dream. His brain is incapable of creating a vision that can compete with the dread that not sleeping brings.

Tonight is a very good night. It lets him both sleep soundly and dream beautifully. He's in the cottage; and he's not alone. Helen's there too. He can hear her moving around the house. Boiling water for tea, taking a shower. He can't see her. That's the trick – he gets to dream of Helen, but not to see her. He accepts it. He is still filled with excitement. It's always the anticipation that really matters. Knowing that at any second the door can open. That Helen would be there, that she could just walk into his arms. It's the closest to happiness that he gets.

Then it starts raining. Then hailing. It's very loud; stifles the sounds of Helen's presence. Adam's annoyed. He shutters the windows and walks across the walls, trying to fade out the outside noise. To listen to Helen. He knows she's still somewhere there, she's still inside the cottage. But he can no longer hear her.

In his last attempt he closes his left ear; presses his right ear to the wall. For a moment he thinks he succeeded. There is an absolute silence. It's so quiet that Adam catches the sound of Helen sneezing. The good old sneezing. Just as the joy overcomes him, someone drills from the other side. Straight to the inside of his ear.

Adam screams, pressing his hands against the ear.

He sits up in his bed, his left hand still pushed against his ear, his face cringing with pain. He remains in this position a few seconds longer, until he realises the ear no longer hurts. He takes his hand off; looks at it. He's prepared to see the skin covered in blood. He forgets that dreams leave no visible traces.

He looks around, recognises his bedroom. Then the noise of drilling that violated his dream resounds again. Adam looks to the door; smiles. The coffee grinder, of course.

He gets up, walks out of the bedroom. He halts the moment he steps outside. The familiar smell fills the apartment. Adam doesn't just inhale it; he stands there to let the smell of coffee saturate his clothes, skin, hair. He can't risk drinking it again; it's one of the small sacrifices he decided to make.

When he finally walks into the kitchen, the coffee grinder is still on. It looks like it's about to explode. He paces towards the machine and switches it off. The metal is boiling hot, the coffee nearly steaming. It probably would've exploded, had he not walked in.

Adam turns to the woman. She stands by the wall, staring in space.

Are you grinding coffee or trying to burn it? Adam says with scorn. The woman only looks at him blankly. Like she doesn't even recognise him; doesn't know who he is. Adam recognises her expression; he knows it all too well. His face reddens with shame.

He tries to smile at the woman; strokes her cheek.

Here, he whispers. Let me handle it.

Adam sets on the coffee machine.

Double shot? he asks.

The woman nods. He fixes his eyes on her face. She is extremely pale, as if all the blood has drained from her face. Her features seem frozen. If a fly now landed on her face, the woman probably wouldn't move. Maybe wouldn't even notice.

THE UNDERGROUND

MARO

The leisure area around the pool transforms during the night. It's not the lights though; these always stay the same. It's the smoke.

Whoever finds their way to the underground, discovers that nothing helps passing the nights away more efficiently than smoking.

Every night, the nocturnals gather around the pool like a bonfire. They rest on the deckchairs; sit by the water. Some wear swimsuits, others cover with robes. A few choose nothing but sunglasses. Each of them holds a cigarette in their hand. The embers lighten up the dim space like shooting stars.

Together the nocturnals burn the night hours away.

Maro looks at his comrades and smiles. Sometimes the underground reminds him of a holiday resort for sinners, opened exclusively at night. It's the only place where they still get to live in the present. To experience something, no matter how insignificant. Taking a break from the past, creating new memories. It's a rare gift. And one that none of them deserves.

For Maro it's also the only time he gets to enjoy the silence. The moment he walks in here and finds the others, he removes the headphones. Human presence replaces the tunes, keeps him safe. Even if no words are spoken, the bodies stay alert to each other. Communicate.

He shares the deckchair with Natasha. Her perfect figure curls up in Maro's arms. He's no longer capable of arousal, or even mild excitement. But he enjoys the feeling of her skin against his. He lies still, with one of his hands placed under his head while the other caresses Natasha's back.

He can sense she's bored. Natasha has been the last one to join them, and she still expects the nights to provide her with entertainment. For the men and women who gather here to try and amuse her.

In some ways Maro admires her entitlement. Neither the building nor sleeplessness succeeded in managing Natasha's expectations. She requires that this place should be just like the rest of the world; serve as her playground.

And even here, Natasha's wish has received certain recognition. Maro's noticed that she has had a mobilising effect on others. When she first entered, they all wanted to step up; rise to the occasion of her company. For that, Maro will always feel both respect and gratitude. He liked seeing that this group of life runaways was still capable of making an effort.

But even beauty such as Natasha's can activate the nocturnals for a limited time only. The dopamine that their midbrains began producing from the first night that Natasha stepped in fuelled them for months. It wasn't just the novelty of her presence, that would've lasted a couple of nights, a week at most. The novelty of her perfection was something that their minds continued failing to familiarise themselves with.

Maro always believed that the brain is the greatest predator. The moment it comes across an unknown, it turns humans into its satellites. It drags their bodies with dopamine to power the investigation. It tricks their hearts to believe there's a reward awaiting at the end of the quest. But it is knowledge alone that the brain is after. Once the novelty wears off, it's game over.

Natasha has been coming here every night since. After months of relentless activity, nocturnals' brains surrendered. They familiarised themselves with her presence and gave up on understanding her beauty. Their bodies have been running on fumes far too long. They needed to break.

Now they gather around the pool like alligators. They have entered the state of hibernation, shutting down all unnecessary functions. Saving the energy. But the moment they smell the prey, they'll know what to do.

Natasha stands up abruptly and walks towards the swimming pool. She halts on the edge; stretches. She is flawless in her nudity. The smoke frames her, as if in preparation for a performance.

No one around seems to notice. Natasha dives into water. The splash fills the otherwise quiet space.

LIV

There isn't much difference between a graveyard and a park. Not when you just look at them from the outset. It's all about what you cannot see; what lies underneath. The underground.

Liv prefers graveyards. She always did. It's mostly about the silence. There are parts of the day and parts of the night when the parks, too, can be quiet. But they're never silent. Not the way the graveyards can be. Instead of ponds and flower beds then, Liv walks around the stones. Sits on marble tombs instead of benches.

To be fair, most of the time she doesn't even know they aren't parks. She walks into graveyards like she is in a hypnosis, drawn by the wilderness of bushes and trees. Even the air there feels different; denser. Like it is layered with the countless number of invisible mouths breathing in, breathing out.

But it used to be something she only ever sensed, and never put in words. Not until Robert observed that all her favourite hideouts were former cemeteries. He thought it morbid. Liv thought it fitting.

She's always liked people and places that put little effort into pleasing her. That exist on their own accord. Don't need her.

And parks are tailored to please. Their only reason for existence is recreation. Leisure. The moment Liv would step in a park, she felt the pressure to enjoy herself.

The opposite is true for graveyards. There she would be a stranger; a trespasser. To walk in, sit down with a book instead of a prayer, was to invade someone's privacy. And where something is kept private, something is to be discovered. Entering a graveyard would give her a thrill familiar to that of stealing other people's stories.

But she's never wished to be buried in a graveyard. She'd rather have a park, or a garden. She imagines that the burial site must be her final destination. She's never believed that she'd die after her body refuses to carry on. But she also cannot conceive of any place she'd rather be heading to. Maybe other people will be going to other places. Heavens, hells. But not her. She knows she will stay right here, in this world. In the afterlife she wishes to retain the same status she has had, that of an outsider. At last invisible, there'll be no limits to her prying. At last she'll know.

Robert hated graveyards. And here he is, on his own demand. Liv is not surprised. We die the way we live. Robert thought life was nothing but suffering. That's why he chose her instead of Sarah. He wanted to hurt and knew that Liv would bring him pain.

She moves slightly to the side to have a better look at the memorial service. She stands at some distance, hidden behind a large oak tree. She knows she shouldn't be here. She doesn't want to cause a scene. Just to get a chance to say her own goodbye.

There is a group of people forming a half-circle. A much larger group than Liv would've expected. She recognises only a few faces. The rest are strangers. She wonders whether it's her who didn't really know Robert or it's the crowd. Have they all gathered here because of the scandal, hungry for a spectacle? She takes a step back, making sure no one sees her.

Sarah stands in the middle. Liv finds it both funny and terrifying that she had to wait until the day of Robert's funeral to take the limelight. It suits her tough. She's always been tailored for a master of ceremonies.

Robert asked for there to be no words spoken, Sarah says with solemnity. Liv feels the sting of this request. She knows that it is how she was expected to react; why the request was made in the first place. To shame her.

He must've known she wouldn't have been able not to be here. He wanted her to hear those words; hear them coming from Sarah.

Liv can picture Robert writing these precise orders. Writing and weeping at the pain he'd be causing her. He knew that to prohibit words was to discredit the only value she's ever had. But he thought it fair; a just pain for the pain she's caused.

She feels angry to be so predictable, to act as orchestrated. Knowing doesn't stop the burning sensation that's putting her skin on fire. No speeches, no condolences, Sarah continues. There is a pause. A middle-aged woman who stands alone, wrapped in a woollen coat, bursts into tears. Liv wonders who she might have been in Robert's life. There is no physical reminiscence; unlikely a relative. Probably a former patient. Fooled to believe his talking saved her marriage; saved her.

Sarah glares at the woman.

No weeping! she reprimands her. Robert asked to be honoured with silence.

Having Sarah must've been a solace in his last hours. Knowing that there's someone who would carry out even the most absurd request in every detail.

Liv wishes she could pity her. But the truth is, she feels jealous. She always did. She envied their friendship, their rapport. That bond they shared. Watching them together she often wondered whether she, too, could one day become more agreeable.

But she wasn't the least surprised he chose her over Sarah.

Being the type of man that Robert was entails making all the wrong choices.

Sarah turns around and picks up a box. The ashes, Liv thinks with dread.

There will also be no scattering of ashes, Sarah announces. Instead, Robert wanted each of you to leave with one of these in your pockets.

She opens the box. From where Liv stands, she cannot see what's inside the box. But Sarah begins walking around the group, distributing whatever it is that Robert decided to leave behind.

Now it's Liv's time to disappear before people start moving and someone sees she's here. I loved you, she whispers her goodbye. It was hard not to. You were beautiful, kind-hearted and brilliant. Sometimes, you were even brave.

It's just too bad all these virtues lay in isolation, she thinks, surprised with the spite that her thoughts reveal. Like those meals served in hip restaurants, she goes on. Great ingredients that fail to make a dish.

That's you, Robert, Liv continues her silent tirade. You had all the parts that could make a great man, but there was no glue that would hold them together.

Liv doesn't realise her thoughts have turned into speech. Not very loud; more of an angry whisper than a cry. But it's enough to draw attention. People grab their phones, start recording, taking pictures.

Liv hardly sees anything. She's consumed with pain but she pretends that it's rage. Only when her eyes meet Sarah's, she breaks down. Weeps.

Sarah paces in her direction. Liv panics. She turns around, about to run away, but Sarah gets there faster. She blocks Liv's path and pushes the box in front of her.

Here, Sarah says. He wanted you to have one.

Liv stares at the box. Sarah opens it. Inside shines a row

of ink cartridges.

What... what is it? Liv asks. It cannot be... she thinks.

Guess, Sarah sniggers. It is, Liv realises as the terror takes over her.

Sarah grabs all the cartridges left in the box and forces them into Liv's hands.

Here, Sarah says. They're all yours.

MARO

Maro's hierarchy of needs retains the classical shape; that of a triangle. It's just a much smaller one. Two thirds of Maslow's pyramid, to be exact.

It started with reducing the basics; sex and sleep. But to cut them out was to deny his physiology. It was possible, he has come to learn. But only if all the remaining needs – breathing, water, food and shelter – were tended to with the greatest care.

He doesn't just breathe; he performs breathing exercises. Every couple of hours his alarm goes off and Maro drops whatever it is he's doing to let the oxygen penetrate his body.

Next comes the hydration. Throughout the day he measures every sip of water until he reaches four litres. From then he continues drinking, just no longer needs to count.

Frequency of food is less relevant. He found out that fasting can be unexpectedly revitalizing. What's crucial though is the type of food he takes in. High energy is a must, but sugar spikes are to be avoided at all costs. He cannot afford crashing.

Last comes the shelter. That's why he's here; no matter how troublesome is their relationship, the building will never deny him refuge.

It's a clear hierarchy of values; each day he knows exactly what to do. Or he used to know, before he had a companion. The sudden appearance of the other, the unexpected human connection introduces a need from a whole different category; that of social belonging. Maro is well aware that he cannot afford satisfying this want. Between physiology and intimacy there is yet another level: safety. And Maro can never feel secure. His life is endangered.

He looks at Liv, resting on the deck chair side by side with him. She wears a wildly colourful swimming suit, which makes her look even more out of place here than usual.

But seriously, why does he call you Helen? Maro starts speaking without making an attempt to turn or look at her.

He can call me anything he likes, Liv shrugs her shoulders. But just like Maro, she stares straight ahead.

Anything but Liv, Maro remarks.

She does not respond and for a while neither of them speaks. Only then Maro turns around. Not to look at her, but to investigate with curiosity.

Are you here to write? he asks.

On the contrary, Liv answers. I'm here to not write.

She sits up and begins to collect her things, getting herself ready to go.

It's a good book, Liv, he says.

Liv freezes and for the first time looks at him.

You're wrong, she says with firmness. It's not a good book. It's a very bad book.

Well, forgive me, but I disagree, Maro says. You're forgetting I, too, read it.

It's not about how it reads, Liv responds. It's about what it does. What it did.

She pauses, unsure whether to continue.

You might laugh... she begins.

I'm not laughing, he whispers back.

She turns to him. Like she cannot simply believe the sounds she hears and needs the image to reassure he's telling the truth.

No, you're not, she admits after a careful investigation.

She looks like she is about to say something else, but then suddenly changes her mind and stands up abruptly.

I better get home.

She begins to walk away.

Liv? Maro calls after her.

She halts and turns around.

Hm?

You'll need a strategy.

What are you talking about? she laughs.

I'm serious. You cannot just not write, he says. It's a compulsion.

How would you know? her voice is filled with sarcasm.

Trust me, he says. Compulsions cannot be simply removed. They've got to be replaced. You must know that. But if you don't, he hesitates.

If I don't?

Well, you'll realise soon enough, he mumbles.

THE OBJECTS
SHE LEFT BEHIND

ADAM

He opens the door with fury. It's been growing for days now, it demands an explosion. It's better this way; too often Adam would suppress it. Let it fester.

That's how he thought a man should behave. Poison himself rather than hurt others. It's not something that he's been taught; at least not by example.

His father was known for his temper. Had he only known how to control himself, she would have stayed; wouldn't have left them. Adam used to believe it was that simple. And so he couldn't forgive his father.

The joke's on him. It was his self-control that drove Helen away, he knows it now.

But he is done with being nice. And Alice should be the first to know.

Why her, it's not entirely clear. Adam tells himself that she's the one who triggered the rage. What he doesn't tell himself is that she is also the only one who would let him get angry; sit through his outburst. Alice is the only person who has ever loved him. Adam realises that it makes her indispensable.

Today he believes that Alice deserves his fury. He's never paid much attention to her words, barely heard them. But that sentence about Adam living with a stranger sunk deep inside him. She meant it like a warning. As if he didn't know what he was doing; he simply got tricked. Again.

He's tried to brush it off; not pay attention. But every day Alice's words have weighed heavier, making it harder to fall asleep by the woman's side. That is something he cannot forgive. No one had the right to take his sleep away. So now he storms into Alice's office, for the first time opening a closed door unannounced. No knocking to which she could respond, no invitation for him to come inside.

It surprises Adam how much he enjoys it, that feeling of breaking in. It carries him across the room. He needs all his resolve to halt by her desk; to stop himself from walking behind it. For now he doesn't want to think what could have happened if he didn't.

Exactly a year ago I woke up to find that a woman I've been living with for years is gone, he says.

Alice blinks rapidly.

On a Tuesday morning. Tuesday morning, Alice! he says and hits his flat palms against the surface of her desk.

She jumps up in her seat; stops blinking. Maybe she's realised that he's here not to have a conversation; it's a performance. Adam doesn't need her to understand. He needs her to listen.

Who the fuck leaves on a Tuesday?! Adam shouts. Alice knows better than to try responding.

Her compliance takes away his edge. The high is over, now he's crushing. It's not just the memories that start hurrying in. It's the feelings they trigger.

Adam leans over the desk, pressing his hands against the surface for extra support. He needs to regroup; he's not done yet.

It's as though she wanted to do it on Monday, he begins, embarrassed at how fragile his voice sounds. To have a fresh start, he continues nevertheless.

But then... she just couldn't bring herself to. She'd always been a real coward, hadn't she? he sniggers. It's a horrible sound, this evil laugh. He'd rather not know which part of him it came from.

Who else would leave like that, in the middle of the night, without a word? he asks gently, as to cover up the moment of disgrace. And this time his question is an invitation.

She didn't leave a note, did she? Alice asks.

What a fucking difference would a note make?! But no, she didn't even care enough to write a damn post-it! Adam pauses to calm down his breath. It's as though she thought I might have not noticed, he continues, making his voice sound gentle again. Oh boy, have I noticed! Adam laughs quietly, as if to himself. But his laughter is a part of the performance; it's all for her.

Adam knows that all she wants now is to reach across the desk and stroke his face. He takes long enough for her to not only imagine doing it, but how it'd feel if she dared touching his skin.

But you know what? he says. The first five minutes of laying alone in bed seemed more real than the years of sleeping side by side with her. As though I was expecting it and things were finally as they were supposed to be.

Alice sits quietly, leaning forward. She's soaking in his words. Their faces are very close, nearly touching. He can smell the excitement slowly making its way to the surface of her skin; evaporating through the pores.

See, her presence by my side never felt quite right, like finding a bag full of money and hiding it in your closet, he drawls, letting each word make its own entrance. Then he falls quiet; straightens up.

He starts walking towards the door. He's not done, not yet. He wants his final words to resound, to stay with her when he leaves. Once he reaches the door, he turns back to face her.

That Tuesday when I woke up in an empty bed I realised it makes no difference how much time you spend with someone. We never really know each other. Like it or not, we all live with strangers.

So you say now, Alice responds unexpectedly, like a statue that suddenly comes to life. I don't know, Adam, she says, shaking her head gravely. It seems to me you're asking for trouble.

LIV

The pen cartridges shimmer in Liv's hand. A bunch of bullets, masquerading as jewels.

Liv sits very close to the window, as if to catch the glow from the outside. She avoids switching on the electric lights until Adam comes home. They're different here than anywhere else she's ever been. So bright and sterile; laboratory lights. Make her feel like a specimen in a social experiment.

She leans forward. In the evenings the windows finally change from opaque to clear, letting her look outside.

Liv's like a camera. To stay sane, she needs to watch, record. She believes in the power of documentation.

But during the day the order seems reversed; it is she who feels watched. Not just by the residents; that wouldn't be anything that unusual. But here the main surveillance is by the building in which she's an intruder. A trespasser. It is being checked that she does no harm.

She is a little surprised, but not bothered by, the lack of interest in her. But she is staggered by the reverence that everyone gives to the Estate. There is nothing to record here; during the day there are hardly any people. And if she manages to spot someone; they're in the middle of running from one place to another.

Liv knows from Adam that all the apartments are occupied. She had heard before she had stepped behind the gate that the Estate is among the most sought after addresses in the province. An architectural marvel just outside the city; you need approval to be let in. Exclusive, like a club.

To Liv, the criteria of admission remain a mystery. There are those who rule the world, those who failed. And those who never have done and never will do anything extraordinary. Like Adam, Liv thinks with contempt.

This exclusive address feels like a facade. The residents

don't seem to really live here; they all dwell among the empty, hostile walls that refuse to be claimed. Even Maro's situation appears tentative. After all these years, it still looks like he's crashing here.

Liv feels as though she found herself in the middle of a film set. That part doesn't bother her, it actually makes it easier. All she needs to stay here is to play her part.

Ta da! Adam's voice unexpectedly breaks the silence. And the darkness, since the light switches on like it had a sound sensor. Maybe it does. Maybe it just got one right now. Liv begins to think that the rules and the workings of the Estate are mutable.

She takes a moment before she turns to Adam. She wants to make sure there is not a trace of irritation left on her face. She breathes in. She might even try decorating herself with a smile.

She hears Adam walking across the room towards her. He must be excited; usually he just stands there, waiting for her reaction to his presence. He might be plain, but he's not stupid. He seems to understand that to her living with him still means living with a stranger. Maybe it's the same for him; he doesn't seem bothered by their lack of familiarity. For some reason he needs her by his side. In exchange he remains discreet, tactful. She might not be able to sleep but he makes sure that she gets the space to breathe.

She turns around just as Adam halts in front of her. She now understands the excitement. Adam brought her a gift. A large carton rests on his forearms, like an offering.

Liv looks at the box. It contains a laptop. The moment her eyes recognise the familiar shape, they bounce off it like tennis balls.

Adam steps closer, stretching out his arms in her direction.

For you, he says with uncertainty. No doubt he noticed her reaction, but it must look so irrational that even someone like Adam doesn't instantly give up.

I thought it might entertain you a bit while I'm at work? He tries again, speaking in a tone of voice one would use with a spoiled child.

It has nothing to do with her whimsy, her temper. She cannot force her head to turn and look back.

Adam bends forward and squeezes her shoulder.

Are you ok? he asks with a mixture of irritation and concern.

She thinks that if she fixed her eyes on Adam's face and kept them there, very still, she might be safe. She might be able to block out the thought of what he's holding.

Liv slowly shifts her head. Her eyes meet Adam's. They're so close to hers, and there is no way out, nowhere else she can look. She knows too well that such proximity very quickly results in intimacy; something neither of them needs, something they managed to avoid until now.

I'm fine, she says. And thank you. So sweet of you to think about this.

You're welcome, Adam nods, unconvinced. He seems surprised by the intensity of her gaze, maybe even finds it uncomfortable. But it triggers a small dose of curiosity. Adam is not interested in Liv, she knows that. She also knows that he is a resolute man who wants to keep track of new data that might affect his situation. He now studies her carefully, trying to find a reason why her words contrast her behaviour.

You sure you're all right? he asks. I thought it'd make you happy...

It does! Liv exclaims with as much enthusiasm as she's capable of producing. I'm just a little tired, that's all.

The magic phrase, the command that every time forces Adam to wriggle and change the subject. It shuts him out yet again.

Still having troubles sleeping? Adam asks nervously,

standing up. It's a rhetorical question, and he is already walking out, neither expecting nor wanting to hear the answer. He drops his rejected gift in the corner just before he exits. An elephant in the room. More a snake than elephant, really.

ADAM

The woman has her back turned to him. She's awake, but she has been awake every night since she moved in here. What worries Adam is that she lays completely still. Normally she wriggles, tosses and turns, sits up, lies down, stands up again.

All this movement never bothers him; on the contrary, it lets him sleep. It is that soundtrack of human presence by his side that makes him feel safe.

But tonight she is motionless. The thought of her dead doesn't enter his mind; even without a single movement or sound, the woman's presence in the bed remains very alive. Her body radiates unnatural heat, her smell is particularly sharp. Stress must make her sweat more, filling the room with acidity.

That's how Helen was the night before all the problems started, he suddenly remembers. And now it is he who starts sweating. It can't be, he thinks. Not again. Not now when he just started recovering.

He doesn't dare to turn her around. Instead, he lifts himself up on his forearms, hoping to catch her reflection in the unshuttered window.

And there it is. Eyes wide open, a fist stuck in her mouth, teeth clenching around it. Tears run down her face steadily, rhythmically, as if there were two gutters attached to her eyes. Adam can't be sure whether she knows he is watching her. If so, she does not let on.

MARO

The light is exceptionally warm tonight. It drips from the walls like honey, making the air denser. The change in the light affects the way they move, like film characters played in a slow-motion. The smoke blurs the contours of their faces, their features smudge. Maro thinks that the light here might be a filter that makes them all look more authentic; as if the degradation has already taken a physical form.

But then he walks closer to the pool where Natasha swims on her back. She never bothers to wear a swimsuit, or anything at all. She takes off her clothes the moment she steps into the underground. It's a part of a performance, as if she was releasing herself from a bondage that was wrapped around her by those with whom nature was less generous.

From up close Natasha's physicality is as flawless as the day she moved in here. It's as if the sleep deprivation has left no mark on her, maybe even added a final touch to her grandeur. She's not just perfect. She's a woman with a secret, a dark side.

As Natasha moves closer to the pool's edge, Maro notices that her porcelain skin seems to glow in the dark. The water frames her, adding a touch of green to her blue eyes, turning them in a pair of large turquoises. She's the night blooming flower; the evening primrose of the underground world, the dragon fruit.

But there's no one here left to marvel at her glory. The rest of them don't take the sleeplessness with grace. All they want, all they can afford to want, is to pass through yet another night.

Maro turns away from the pool. If he stares at the swimming Natasha for too long the image might hypnotise him; he might start deluding himself of the splendour in their fortune.

He looks around, sobering up quicker than he might've

44

wished.

Sergei, Anna and Luca sit together around a stool that serves as a poker table. There's little glamour in their appearances, unless one was into asylum chic. Sergei wears a bathrobe that has seen better times. The once fine fabric tattered; it has now become unintentionally see-through. And what Maro sees underneath Sergei's bathrobe is yet another fabric; equally frayed. Sergei's skin hangs off his bones like an old, oversized body suit.

That's what happens with the body of a chronic insomniac. It remains under continuous, severe stress, producing too much cortisol, and cortisol then destroys collagen. The skin ages; sags. Sergei doesn't mind his body fading. On the contrary, he indulges in watching its decline. That's his aesthetics; he finds destruction the essence of sublime.

Others have preserved more vanity, and it is in turn the vanity that keeps them better preserved. Those have found ways to cope, reduce stress. Maro exercises. Thea and Titus relentlessly make love. Alex meditates, often for hours at a time. Sometimes he meditates instead of coming here.

Natasha doesn't need a strategy; her body never seems to give into stress. She probably cannot conceive of a situation that could be potentially dangerous; of anyone wanting to cause her harm. Beauty makes you feel invincible, Maro can see that.

Then there are Anna and Luca. Neither of them bothers to put up a fight with time. Anna's too old; she cannot wait to vanish. She sinks herself in sweatpants and an oversized t-shirt. The selection that reflects exactly how much she values her own presence.

Luca's too young; the possibility of decay hasn't occurred to him yet. Tonight he wears swim briefs. But it isn't coyness that prevents him from dropping all his garments, the way Natasha does. Luca enjoys dressing up his body; decorating it. He loves fashion; sees his body as a perfect frame for the pieces he selects.

Next to them are Thea and Titus. They lie together on a deckchair, hugging each other. Both of them wear identical black swimsuits. Their looks are always curated as to make them look indistinguishable. It's intended as a demonstration of their unity. But Maro knows that a need to parade their togetherness hides a tragedy; an essential incompatibility. It takes a lot of energy to put up such a perfect show, night after night. For now they don't mind. But it might change, and when it does, there will be little left to rescue.

Maro steps away from the pool and walks up to an empty deckchair. He takes out Liv's book; he marked few passages he wanted to return to. He sits down with his legs up, making himself comfortable. He will rest among them. For better or worse, they're his people.

Sounds of acoustic guitar begin filling the underground. Bad sounds; Maro's not sure whether someone is tuning the guitar or actually tries to play it.

He looks up. Alex sits on the edge of the pool, messing around with the instrument.

Maro's about to intervene, but Natasha's quicker. She emerges from the pool right by the place where Alex sits, making sure she splashes as much water at him as she only can. She then stands by him, shaking the water off like a dog.

But Alex doesn't mind; he laughs it off. He puts the guitar away and jumps into the pool himself. Natasha snorts and looks away. Her eyes immediately meet Maro's, brighten up. She always enjoys having an audience.

Natasha swiftly crosses the room and lands on his lap. She kisses him hello. It's a strong, warm kiss on the lips. But it lacks even a trace of desire; a possibility of affection. It's a kiss of an android, Maro thinks. Still, Natasha's human and her wet skin is getting cold. She trembles. Maro wraps his arms around her and rests Natasha's head on his chest. He rubs his hands against her body to warm it up.

Thea turns to them with curiosity, hungry to find evidence of their passion. She's accepted romance is off the cards but cannot conceive of total absence of lust. There it is though; both Maro and Natasha are perfectly closed off on another. There isn't an open pore in their bodies through which one could get under the other's skin. Thea sighs and turns on her back.

I'm bored, she barks, annoyed. Seemingly the complaint is addressed to no one in particular. But Maro knows it is he from whom everyone here expects an answer. He likes it this way; it's the only remnant of the man he once used to be. A man with answers.

He now gently moves Natasha's head and lifts himself up on the forearms. He looks up to Thea.

How about a game? he asks, like a father would ask a daughter. Amused at her annoyance, while hiding his amusement to avoid her rage.

I love games! Anna exclaims, clasping her hands like she was a ten, not a sixty-years-old.

Let's play dirty secrets, Luca says, smiling sleazily.

We already know all of each other's secrets, Thea snorts.

Last dreams? Sergei asks, genuinely interested. He has a theory that last dreams carry a message as to why they were the last. If one could decipher it, one could sleep. So far no one has succeeded.

Depressing, Anna responds, gently reminding him of the past failures. She was one of those who believed Sergei's theory might hold; one of those who stepped in here with hope.

How about daydreams? Alex asks, in an attempt to lighten the atmosphere. He's got out of the pool already and walks towards the pile of towels to dry himself.

Disturbing? Thea says. And she's right. Those who do not sleep lose the right to fantasise.

I know, I know! Titus enthusiasts. He hardly ever gets any idea of his own. Thea, significantly older, is the spokesperson of their duet. When Titus finds among his thoughts one worth sharing, his excitement cannot be ignored. Everybody turns to him. Their interest in what he is about to say is moderate, but they envy him nevertheless. To have something, anything, that makes you that alive is a rarity.

Titus enjoys this moment in the limelight. He does not want to rush through it; takes his time. Once he satiates his hunger for their attention, he begins speaking.

The first dreams we want to have, he says. They look at each other unsure whether they are to feel insulted. Has he really just mocked them; ridiculed? But no, Titus's eyes radiate innocence. And hope.

Devastating, Maro says after a while. One by one they turn their heads away, careful as to avoid meeting each other's eyes during this retreat. Then each of them returns to whatever else they have been doing. Natasha gets up and jumps back into the pool. Luca deals cards; Sergei loses the money that Anna then wins. Thea strokes Titus's face. He doesn't understand what just happened, what he did wrong. But Thea coaxes him to not think about it; she shifts his attention to her body instead. They all make sure to behave exactly as if this conversation never took place. It never had a right to take place.

Only Alex walks up to Maro. Drying his head with a towel, he sits at the edge of his deckchair. Liv's book falls on the floor.

We need a new game, Alex warns, picking up the book and handing it to Maro.

No, Maro responds, fixated on the cover of Liv's book. His face brightens up. How did he not think about it earlier?

Not a new game, Maro says. Just a new player.

LIV

She's about to knock on the door when she sees it has been left ajar. She pushes it; a shaft of blue light and a stream of dance music spill onto the corridor.

Hello? Liv says. Loudly; she hopes she'll be asked to step in.

There is no response. Liv hesitates, then pushes the door and walks in.

Maro? she calls, unsure what to expect. When walking in uninvited, one rarely makes pleasant discoveries. She passes by a large open space which she supposes might have been intended as a living room. Now it resembles more of a gym area. There are mats, weights, a punching bag. No wonder Maro has retained such great form, despite his age.

She follows the music and walks into his bedroom. Again, it's a guess; the room has no distinguishable features, no furniture. Liv spots a rolled up mat in the corner. Maro must be using it to rest.

Liv suddenly thinks how differently Adam's and Maro's apartments feel. They're both unfurnished; if anything, it is Adam's apartment that complies with at least basic standards. A bedroom has a bed in it; a living room a sofa. But Maro's place has a lived-in feeling. It's not a home; Liv has come to believe the Estate wasn't built to give anyone a home. But Maro's apartment makes for a solid shelter.

Adam's apartment, on the contrary, feels more like a hallway. Like one was always waiting there for something else to happen. Or dreaming of another place, another time. Left behind or shimmering ahead, somewhere in the far distance.

But both apartments are part of the Estate; there is more to them that meets the eye. Something has been undone there, Liv c an sense it. The floors, walls and windows might be bare, but there's something creeping from underneath.

Just as the thought crosses Liv's mind, she senses a change in the room. It feels as if she was no longer alone here; something has woken up.

She turns around, ready to leave. Then her eyes catch a sight of an opened box in the corner of the room. Her box, now opened. The temperature in the room jumps up rapidly to an unbearable level. As if she had stepped into a dry sauna. She struggles to breathe; she needs to get out. But just as she passes by the box, the room gets chillingly cold.

The building often does; it plays with lights, with temperature. She should be getting used to it. She'll have to, if she wants to stay.

This moment is as good as any other to stop letting the building direct her steps. She resolves she will stay here no matter how uncomfortable. She will only leave when the temperature becomes truly unbearable.

To take her mind off the cold she decides to look at the box. She crouches, reaches inside it. She doesn't dare to pick one of the books; not yet. For now, she runs her hand against the row of sleek covers, imagines how they might look. She remembers how much she loved the design that she was sent. She only ever saw it on the screen, never in print.

Would it be really all that terrible if she now had a look? She still resents the book. But it's the content she dreads; her own words. The cover is a whole different matter. She didn't author it. It is somebody else's work and it deserves recognition.

She picks up a copy and bring it closer to her chest. She holds it there for a moment, like she was cradling a baby. She opens it, almost involuntarily. She was supposed to only look at the cover. She cannot resist; should she even have to? It's her book.

Liv tenderly runs through the pages. Her fingers stroke the lines, gently follow the shape of the letters. They're hers; it is through her that they came to be.

Suddenly she shuts the book. She fooled herself again; let herself be seduced. She's hopeless; she'll never change.

Liv runs out of the bedroom. As she passes by the gym area she notices that all the windows are open. She halts for a second. The freezing air that blows from the outside explains the sudden temperature drop. But the windows in the Estate never open. Safety reasons, Adam explained when she just moved in.

Liv slowly turns back to the door. She begins walking; she doesn't dare to run. It's an instinct. When face to face with a wild creature, a rapid movement can become deadly. That's what this building is, a beast.

She hears the windows shutting, one by one. Like they were beating out the rhythm for her steps. Or erasing the traces of her intrusion.

The moment she gets back to the corridor, her steps pick up the pace. She still walks, much quicker, as quickly as she can. She notices that every door she passes by is left ajar. She knows she shouldn't look. But she's got an in-built camera in her brain. She must look.

She realises that all the apartments look exactly the same. Empty.

She walks down the stairs. She needs to slow down; the steps appear shorter and steeper than when she was coming up just half an hour before.

She manages to get back to get back to Adam's apartment. She goes straight to the living room, towards the box. The second box that's been gifted to her lately.

In few swift jerks she manages to tear up the carton. She takes out the laptop and smashes it against the wall. Once, twice, ten times.

She looks around, notices her rejected painting hiding in the corner of the room.

There might be no nails in the house, but Adam still keeps a hammer. Why he keeps it, she didn't ask.

With the hammer in her hand, she goes to the kitchen. She picks up a knife with the sharpest blade and a thick handle. She returns to the living room; she knifes the picture to the wall.

She's not worried about noise. She knows by now; nothing wakes up Adam. And everybody else is just like her. Nobody else ever sleeps.

ADAM

He wakes up alone, spread out all across the bed. But these days he's not worried; he knows the woman is still here. Her midnight departure from the bed has become a part of their routine; she leaves as soon as he falls asleep. Like he was a child she was putting to bed.

Adam's body is getting used to having all the space for itself. It's the first time, really. When Helen moved in, the arrival of the bed marked the beginning of their life together. It was he who grew fond of it. With time, Helen came to resent it.

It was then that he got her the sofa; each was to have furniture of their own. But Helen preferred the bathtub. It was closer to how she felt, she explained. Sofa was to rest, to retreat. Helen didn't feel like taking a break. She felt like drowning.

The woman likes the sofa. It makes Adam feel good; it shows his foresight. After Helen left, there were no reasons for him to keep the furniture. He could have thrown them away, together with all her other belongings. He couldn't have known he would ever need them again; couldn't have hoped. And yet a part of him knew; a part of him hoped.

Now that part triumphs. There is a woman in his living room using the sofa. Adam suspects Helen was right; the woman likes it because it reflects how she feels. The woman feels like resting. He lets her do just that.

His favourite part about waking up alone is staying in bed for another five, ten minutes. He's not yet awake; he's half-asleep, half-awake. He inhales the smell of sleep, the smell of his own body sleeping. In the city people rush to open the windows and chase away the night's odour.

No one would do it in the Estate. The windows here don't open; they don't need to. No one here is meant to sleep. But Adam does.

The wave of gratitude towards the woman diminishes his anger about last night. The only person he should be angry with is himself. He got the computer out of guilt; he struggled with the image of her nights and days with absolutely nothing to do. It would have killed Adam. And it's in his interest to keep the woman alive. To keep her here, with him.

But he must not impose his standards on her. He knows little about her; it's a mutual agreement they made the night they met. He should respect it, not try to second guess her needs. If she wanted something, she would've said. Adam has no right to expect appreciation for unrequested gifts. He will stick with making her morning coffee instead. For that she's always been thankful.

He jumps out of bed and walks to the living room. His eyes automatically shift to the sofa; that's where he's used to finding her. But now the sofa is empty.

It only takes a split second for the adrenaline to flood his body. His breath shortens as if there wasn't enough air around him. He wants to bring his hands to his chest, to calm it down. The hands shake so much he struggles to have any control over their movement. He feels dizzy, collapses on the floor.

And that's where he finds the woman. On the floor, eye to eye with him. She looks straight ahead. She doesn't look at Adam, she looks past him. There are pieces of the broken laptop all around her.

The moment Adam sees that the woman is still here, his

breath stabilizes. The tingling sensation in his hands is also gone.

He sits up; he needs a perspective to better understand what just happened here. There are no other clues to be found, only the woman framed by pieces of the broken laptop.

Then Adam notices the knife. A bit further away, by the wall. He tries to stand up but struggles to keep his balance. He feels entirely worn out. Nothing unusual though; he had a panic attack just a few minutes ago. His brain went on an overdrive; needs to rest now.

Adam collects himself and slowly walks up towards the knife. He picks it up; turns to the woman.

What do you need this one for? he asks.

Even though she hears him, Adam needs to wait for a while before she decides to turn in his direction. Then a while longer before she manages to do so. But once her eyes focus on the knife, once they recognise it, she's up on her feet in a split second.

Adam never saw her running before; he wouldn't have guessed she was capable of such speed. Before he understands what's happening, the woman is by the wall. She places both her hands against the flawless, bare surface. She moves them from left to right, and back to left again.

She starts laughing. At first it's just a chuckle, but with every movement of her hands pressing against the wall, the laughter gains resonance. Soon she's cackling; a violent, dreadful sound. It makes Adam want to quiet her, to smash her head against the wall, press her face against the sofa. He doesn't want to know what it is that she finds that amusing, he just wants her to stop.

But he doesn't know how to talk to her; he never had to. Silence has been the backbone of their rapport. It's better then to leave her; things like this often tend to sort themselves out over time. She might be all back to normal by the time he's back from work.

He takes the knife with him, just in case.

His departure to work is backed by Liv's laughter. By then it sounds more like a cry, a fit of hysteria. There is a part of Adam that's impressed by the woman's vitality. For someone who doesn't sleep, she's preserved a great physical strength.

He walks through the gate. The air around him instantly changes. It's not a metaphor, but neither is it anything metaphysical. Everything in the universe is made out of energy; science has long confirmed that. Even the atoms are nothing more but ridiculously tiny energy whirlpools; they never stop spinning and vibrating.

The Estate is then built of unique atoms that radiate a deep sense of purpose. Unlike the energy of the city, outside the gate the energy is scattered and chaotic. Only behind the walls one can sense the presence of intelligent design. Everything here feels directed, intentional.

Adam has no time to dwell on who might be directing it. He always found such idle pondering of no use at best, and often rather harmful. Instead, he tries to reap the benefits of being part of such a masterful system. He matters here. Everyone matters here. They are hand-picked, selected. The energy of the Estate draws them in; the Estate and its residents need to match. He enjoys noticing how many things he and the Estate have in common, as if their natures were aligned. Take the fondness of clear surfaces. It's not a preference here. It's a necessity.

Back in his city days he often felt superfluous; unnoticed. The moment he moved into the Estate he knew he was being watched; everything he did, every step he took was counted. At last he was seen; at last he was significant.

He enjoys now his daily ventures back into the city. He smiles at his fellow commuters, people he passes on the street, his colleagues from the office; it's a smile of triumph.

They're all drifting in search of home, whereas Adam doesn't need a home; he has been chosen to belong to a place.

Adam walks into his office. He sits behind a perfectly clear desktop, begins his work. He struggles to concentrate, despite the hours-long sleep he got last night. It's the anxiety. He's worried about the woman, of what she might do. 'You're looking for trouble,' Alice's words replay in his head.

He stands up rapidly, knocking down his chair. Alice. She's the one who questioned his decision; she might've been right all along.

Adam goes straight to her office but she must have taken a break. He finds Alice in the kitchen, making a coffee there.

This Friday, Adam fires at her.

What about it? she asks, genuinely confused. But her eyes light up the moment she notes Adam's presence.

You've got plans? he responds with a question.

Not yet, no, she says carefully. There is a trace of excitement hovering, ready to take over her face. She's wary not to give into it too quickly. She tries to read him first.

Come over for dinner, he says. The excitement doesn't vanish, but its nature changes. She knows now that the invitation has nothing to do with the two of them; could she really still hope that it ever would? Adam finds it endearing. More, he can relate to it. Both are relentless in their affections; both seem doomed to misdirect them.

The anticipation Alice now experiences has nothing to do with their romantic prospects. Still, there's a thrill of a shared intimacy. Something important just happened in Adam's life, and she is the one he wants involved. Maybe he even needs her.

Something happened! she exclaims. She doesn't need an answer; she's happy to be allowed to read his face. Something bad...

Adam bites his lip; looks away. He's ready to hand her

that little victory.

Just come over for dinner, ok? he says.

MARO

The bench is uncomfortable, like everything else in the Estate. It looks stylish, elegant; but it is not designed to let you rest. Maro came to fully appreciate this side of the Estate soon after he moved in. He arrived guilt-ridden, haunted by his past. But with every week his remorse was overshadowed by the fatigue, which by then had become chronic. Somewhere else his body would have defeated him, muted the guilt. Not here, though. Wherever he turned, he was reminded that he was not to feel comfortable. This was no place to settle. In a way then, the building has come to his rescue.

With time Maro has learned various tricks; just like the incessant stream of music pouring through his headphones. Today his body fights hard for its dosage of microsleep. The music is as loud as ever; the loudest it can be. Still, his eyes keep closing. Every time he manages to reopen them, he makes an attempt to turn the music just a little bit louder. But there is no louder.

Then Liv appears in front of him. He didn't see her approaching; didn't hear her walking towards him. His senses must be more muffled than he suspected.

You're right, she says. I need a strategy.

Maro looks up, trying to focus his vision. Liv stands in front of him, with a clenched fist right above Maro's lap.

For a moment Maro thinks he might get punched. He tilts his head so as to avoid the approaching strike. But Liv opens her fist. A cascade of objects falls down onto his lap..

What are these?! Maro exclaims.

The objects she left behind, Liv says with glowing eyes. She doesn't take her eyes from the collection; doesn't look at Maro. He understands it's a ritual; a literary baptism. She has named them; they have just come to be.

Maro looks at Liv until she turns back to him. He nods, wants her to know that he approves. He picks up an earring.

Tell me about it, he demands.

It's an earring, Liv says.

I wouldn't have guessed...Maro snorts. Seriously, Liv, if you want it to work, you'll have to do better than that.

She doesn't look pleased; Liv's not someone used to being reprimanded. But she hears him; swallows the criticism.

It's Helen's earring, she says after a while.

Aha! Now we're talking! he cheers. He'd hoped that's where she was heading. He didn't know whether she'd dare, whether she'd have it in her.

Where did she get it? he urges Liv to continue.

She didn't, Liv responds.

How come? he asks.

She stole it, Liv says with audacity. Maro can see how much she indulges in saying these words; in telling Maro her story.

So she's a thief, Maro says. His eyes spark as he fights a smile.

No, not a thief, Liv disagrees. But she's confused, she didn't expect this word. It often happens; people dislike thinking that their actions have the power to define them. He watches Liv thinking how to get herself out of this.

Not a real one, anyway, she finally decides. She doesn't need the things she steals.

So why would she do it? he asks.

To protect them, she answers.

Protect who? Maro insists.

Protect what, she corrects him. Clearly now the story has fallen into place. Liv's ready to explain; defend it if needed.

The objects, Liv continues. She saves them from

belonging to someone who wouldn't know how to appreciate them.

So she's a hero, Maro says. There is an undertone of irony, but he makes sure to keep it very light; hardly detectable.

No, just an aesthete, Liv says with solemnity. She seems determined to dismiss his teasing.

It hurts her to think that beautiful things could belong to awful people, Liv goes on with her tale. So she doesn't steal them. She removes them from public view. Limits their availability.

I see, Maro responds. But just to say something; he's mesmerised. It's the first time he sees Liv immersed in something different than watching others. He wishes she could just stand here forever, telling him stories. Liv seems oblivious to the effect that she suddenly has on him.

She would give them back, happily, she adds with excitement. Had she only known they would be in the right hands.

Maro picks up the earring from his lap. He gently fixes it on Liv's ear.

Seems as though they couldn't find a more perfect place, he mumbles. But it's an error; he sees it right away. Something in Liv's face changes. She's finished her story, she's back to paying attention. She smiles at him, but it's not a pleasant smile. It's predatory. Maro realizes with this one gesture he lost the status which his indifference had previously earned him. Before he was unlike anyone else she's met; now he's just like the rest.

So Helen and Liv are not too far apart, ha? he says quickly; too quickly. His tone is playful, but there is a trace of aggression hiding behind the joke.

She says nothing, just raises her eyebrows expectantly. Very well then, he will continue.

Both like to take things away from others? Maro

elaborates.

Liv frowns. Now she's angry; insulted. She wants to run away, half-turns. She notices her collection, still spread across Maro's lap. She cannot leave without it. But to take it would be to demonstrate that Maro is right. He watches her hesitate. She tries to ignore him, but then gives in. The moment their eyes meet, they both chuckle.

Don't be mad, he says, grabbing her hand. We seem to be kindred spirits.

What are you saying? That you, too, are a thief? she asks, pouting. But she doesn't take her hand away. She is like a little girl now. Maybe that's the secret behind her cruelty: she's never really grown up. A woman-child. Maro needs to tread carefully. He decides to say nothing.

It's a smart move. Liv sits down, stretching out her legs and looking ahead of her.

Oh, don't tell me you're a writer... she adds sarcastically. Maro knows she is trying to provoke a reaction. She's not one to take being ignored lightly.

A criminal, Maro then says.

What kind of criminal? she asks playfully.

A murderer, he says. I take away the most precious thing. Life.

Liv sighs, shaking her head dismissively. She's disappointed, he can see it. She was hoping to have him confess but he seems to be joking around instead.

Maro, too, sighs in response; how much he would've wished that was the case.

Oh yeah? Liv says with perfect indifference. And whose life did you take away?

Maro turns to Liv. He wants to be facing her when he utters the words out loud.

My wife's, he says. He watches Liv's face, waiting for her reaction. But she remains still; her face impenetrable. She doesn't look away; and neither does she blink.

LIV

The dress fits her like a glove; second skin. Maro's right; Helen and Liv are not too far apart.

Helen, Liv says to the reflection in the mirror. The woman's features morph slightly, her lips have become fuller, her cheekbones more pronounced. Liv has the face of a retro doll; tiny lips with well defined cupid's bow and a pair of large round eyes. But the woman in the mirror is all grown-up; her eyes narrower, almost almond shaped. The face seems elongated, with sharper contours and pale, thin skin.

Liv scavenges her collection of Helen's accessories; the objects she left behind. She picks up an earring, paints her lips, inserts a golden hairpin. The hairpin is her totem; a few red hairs have been caught between the metal tongs. Liv doesn't remove them; she wishes they could turn her own plain curls into flames.

Helen, Liv repeats, running her fingers across this new face of hers. It might be the lack of sleep; she's been losing a significant amount of weight. She hardly gets any sunshine, any exercise. She hasn't been outside for days. And yet, she's been feeling better lately, stronger. Like her body has adjusted to this new rhythm. To the new place. She doesn't even feel that tired, only muted. Like she is underwater. The sounds, colours and smells are muffled.

Like now; she hears Adam speaking in the other room. He's on the phone, his voice resonates across the apartment. It's loud enough for her to hear the conversation. But she cannot understand the words, cannot distinguish between them.

Liv wonders whether it should start worrying her; whether she can trust herself on how serious her condition is. She turns away from the mirror; away from the woman. She goes to the corridor, determined to decipher Adam's speech.

Yes, one minute, Adam says to the phone. She can hear and understand every word. She's relieved. Her senses might not be as sharp as before but there is no need for emergency. She is about to retreat; she cannot conceive that Adam's conversation could be worth eavesdropping. She turns around and hears him say: Just got to find a pen.

Liv freezes

Adam's voice is so polite; so composed. He crosses the room, enters the kitchen. The kitchen is the only space with drawers. Drawers have pens and paper. Or had, before Liv moved in.

She listens to Adam's movements; notices how frantic they become. Something falls. The drawers and cupboard doors are shut more noisily than necessary; slammed.

Liv walks into the living room to make sure she hears the end of the conversation.

No, still here, Adam responds to the person on the other side. His voice remains calm, but Liv can hear the undertone of fury waiting to explode. She's never seen Adam angry; not really. Annoyed, frustrated; yes. Resentful even. But she has never witnessed an outburst of his temper. She's almost curious to see the eruption; to find out what lies dormant underneath Adam's composure. But she also knows that it's exactly the men like Adam, men trained in self-control, whose fist of anger should be feared. Nothing more dangerous than a nice man who feels he's been repetitively taken advantage of.

She also knows that it's exactly something like this, something meaningless and tiny, which would trigger it. He tolerated the computer; after all it was a gift for her. Whatever she did with it, was none of his concern. But this is different. The pens were his; they belonged to Adam.

I mean, my drawers are normally filled with dozens of pens... Adam mumbles, more to himself than anyone else. Then louder, in a clearer voice, as an attempt to sound jovial:

But you know how it is. Once you need one, they're suddenly all gone!

Then there is the silence; exactly how Liv would've imagined it. She knows he found them. She can visualise the scene; the open drawer, Adam standing still right in front of it. He needs a moment to understand what he's looking at; a graveyard of pens, all broken in half.

I'll call you right back, he says after a while and hangs up.

Liv enters the kitchen; it's best to intervene straight away. It gives her a chance to stir his reaction.

She sees Adam scooping his hand inside the drawer, picking and dropping the corpses of pens.

Adam? Liv says.

Adam doesn't respond; doesn't move. There is no indication that he had even heard her.

Here you are, Liv says gently, stuffing her voice with all the warmth and affection she can still fabricate. She paces to him, places her hands on his shoulders.

Her touch works like a thaw. Adam abruptly closes the drawer and stands up. He turns to face her. Whatever was his intention, it bounces off Liv the moment he sees her. It's the dress, Liv realises. She's forgotten she's had it on; Helen's dress.

She steps back and half-spins. The dress flares out around her.

I thought I should make it up to you for yesterday, Liv says. I really don't know what came over me.

You really don't, do you, Adam snarls unexpectedly.

Liv pauses, alarmed. She anticipated an eruption. She thought there would be swearing, screaming; a hysterical attack even. Not unlike her own the other day. But Adam's poise takes her by surprise. There is something ruthless about it, inhumane even. It also redefines their dynamics; it's a shift of power.

I'm sorry? That's all she can come up with. Her voice

sounds weak, timid. It's a voice of someone prepared to be attacked; hurt.

Adam shakes his head as to dismiss it. Not good enough; he'd expect more from her.

You were saying? he asks, going straight back to the point she was just trying to abandon. He will not let her distract him.

How would you like to make it up to me? he reminds her.

I'm taking you out, Liv says and walks up to him, against the urge to run instead; run away as fast as she can. Strength responds to strength. He's shut her out; there will be no conversation taking place between the two of them tonight. Well then, she must prepare a monologue of her own. She needs it to be good, and she needs it fast.

I thought you didn't want to go out, Adam objects. But just a little bit; just to be consistent. She's got him listening.

Well, I changed my mind, she says with audacity. There is no point in explaining herself; Adam's determined to prove her wrong. But admitted mistakes become powerless, leaving him with no ammunition. I'm allowed to change my mind, right? she asks, just to emphasise her point.

But is she? Said aloud, the question sounds less rhetorical. Adam agrees; that must be why he studies her, unconvinced. Like he was pondering the answer. Whatever it is, he decides not to share it with Liv.

I thought you didn't have any clothes with you, he says instead, pointing to the dress.

I don't, she confirms without taking her eyes off him. Liv sees what Adam is doing; he's resolved to provoke her. But she has resolved not to give in.

They look at each other in silence. It's a weak person's game, Adam, Liv says in her mind. If you want to know something, ask. You will not pressure me to speak otherwise.

Adam is a weak man. A nice, angered, weak man. His aggression can only ever be passive, his attacks indirect, his

64

questions formed as statements. He now looks away; retreats.

It looks pretty good on me, don't you think? Liv says, spinning around in her dress with triumph. She knows it's unnecessary; the teasing. But she can't help it; he really had her scared. She wants to get even, stress the return of her power.

She doesn't realise that it's too quick to parade her victory. She's misjudged his resentment, the scale of his suppressed injury.

Adam jumps towards her. He ignores the dress and instead fastens his eyes on Liv's face. She knows he can see that she's wearing Helen's lipstick.

Adam lifts up his hand to touch Liv's mouth. She notices the stains of ink; feels sick. She doesn't want him to touch her; to stain her.

What happened to your hand? she says, trying to pull away.

Adam does not answer. Maybe he's done answering Liv's questions. Something has come over him. He looks past her. Like she, Liv, wasn't even here. She remembers Liv had not even been invited here. That had been Helen.

Adam's eyes are fixed on Liv's lips. He wipes the lipstick from her mouth with his outer hand. First gently, then more and more violently. The red smudges around Liv's face, blending with ink.

Easy... Liv's voice trembles. She's horrified to realise it's the excitement, not fear, that makes her shake. I won't be able to go out like this, she tries to joke.

We're not going out, Adam says.

He then rips the dress open. He kisses Liv's chest; hungrily, with aggression. She wants not to like it, she really tries. But it must be that hairpin. It puts her head on fire.

VISITORS

ADAM

The doorbell rings twice. The first ring is short; just an announcement of her arrival. The second is significantly longer. Adam imagines that Alice is smiling while she holds her finger the few extra seconds. She wants him to hurry, to feel nervous and rushed. Adam understands it's an attempt to project her anxiety about the visit onto him.

He watched Alice cross the gate twenty minutes ahead of the agreed time. She probably couldn't wait at home any longer and so decided to leave. She must have thought it would be easy to kill time here. To explore the Estate, walk around. Alice and he have known each other for years, but it's the first time he has invited her to come over.

The Estate is not a sight one gets to survey. Being here requires discretion, minding one's own business. Adam saw that the moment Alice looked up, she instantly tripped. And then again, and again, until her attention was reduced to making her way to the entrance safely. Adam checked the time; it was ten to eight. She was still ahead of the agreed time.

She rings the door at a quarter past eight, fifteen minutes late. Adam imagines she must've struggled with the elevator, then gave up, decided to climb the stairs. That could have turned into yet another adventure, for all he knows about the building.

Now Alice is here, ringing the door. Everything is ready, including the woman. Last night brought a change; the woman didn't leave the bed after he fell asleep. She was still awake but stayed there, with him, until morning.

Today she didn't object when he told her about the visit. She even helped him prepare the food; set the table. He picked a new shirt for her, one whose colour best matched the lipstick. It is silently agreed between them that the woman now always wears Helen's lipstick.

Everything is ready then. But Adam doesn't open; not just yet. He stands against the wall, waiting. He wants her to have to ring a third time; to feel unsure about the welcome. He counts in his head; five, ten, fifteen seconds. If she is to ring the third time, it'd be at twenty. He opens the door at eighteen. Alice's hand hangs in the air.

Adam looks at the hand first, then he glares at Alice. Surprise slows down her reactions; she holds her hand long enough for both of them to acknowledge she was just about to ring the door again. It's a tiny thing; a seemingly irrelevant detail. But it is the details in their dynamics that assert his power.

He lets her in. Alice enters, in the random company of odours that she's collected over the hours of preparations before the visit.

She smells of hairspray which fights with traces of shampoo, then there is the body powder and the make-up powder, the lotion, the deodorant and the hand-cream that she's been applying compulsively every hour. All of it crowns a heavily handed application of her new cologne. Adam is certain that she bought it just for tonight; right after she finished work yesterday. She probably left the office earlier. It's a rich oud scent with notes of anise, rosemary and honey. Such a combination crushes a woman like Alice; parodies her.

But she cannot know it; she suffers from anosmia. It's a secret that she hides even from herself, but Adam has known it for years. She's incapable of noticing any scents, distinguishing between them; being attracted or repulsed by the information they carry. Poor Alice, walking around the world unable to smell anything; not even herself. It makes sense for her to want to wrap her body in purchased layers of fabricated aromas, since she cannot trust her own odour.

Adam holds his breath and smiles. She hands him a bottle of wine. He glances over the label. It's an expensive choice;

too expensive for a dinner party between colleagues, close friends even. And it's again a choice that she couldn't have made herself. Alice prefers strong spirits; she knows nothing about wine.

What's her name? Alice whispers, leaning forward.

The amalgamation of smells strikes him across the face, throwing his head to the side. He turns around, remembers he still has the wine in his hands. He could walk a few steps away to put it down; that would give him a chance to breathe. He points out the bottle to Alice and retreats.

Saved from the smell, he's now hit again by the rebounding earlier question. The name; what should he tell her? Adam thought through every detail of this visit; ran through every possible question that Alice could've asked. But here, he forgot the most basic one.

Come on, quick! she rushes him, looking at the door where the woman is. You never told me her name.

Adam looks around nervously.

It's complicated, he evades for now. He needs time to come up with an explanation.

Complicated?! Alice snorts. It's a name, Adam. Things don't get much simpler than that.

He hates when she does it; cuts to the chase with no regard for nuance, complexity. He understands it's a reflection of her own plain structure. But it offends him to be reduced to her standards. It's terrible having to rely on someone like this as his only accomplice.

She didn't say, he admits with reluctance. And immediately hears the absurdity of his situation. He knows it sets the tone for the visit; makes him look desperate, hopeless.

Alice wastes no time pretending she understands; doesn't even try understanding.

So what do you call her? she simply asks.

Helen. I call her Helen.

There is no time for Alice to respond. The woman walks in; she immediately leans on Adam's arm. It's a new gesture; he's unsure whether it's the last night that produced it, or the conversation she might've just overheard. Whatever the cause, its message is clear to all three of them: Alice is not here as Adam's woman. It is she.

The woman seems to enjoy the awkward silence that follows; the silence that her appearance has triggered. She moves her gaze from Adam to Alice and back, smiling. She indulges in those seconds when neither Adam nor Alice know exactly what to do. Adam recognises her triumph; they wanted to treat her like a puppet but it is she who is pulling the strings.

Alice nods. She accepts the defeat; offers the woman her hand.

Nice to finally meet you... she says with an apologetic smile. But just as the woman shakes her hand, Alice adds: Helen. Nice to finally meet you, Helen, she says, accentuating the name to leave no doubt about her take on this entire charade. The woman tries to pull away her hand, but Alice holds on to it firmly.

It's impossible to miss the mockery in Alice's voice. But the woman doesn't even blink. Instead, she plays the part. Unable to free her hand, she puts another hand over Alice's, tightening the grip. She then grins carelessly.

It is, isn't it? the woman says. Adam has not stopped talking about you ever since we met, she looks to Adam; her eyes widening with excitement. He knows he has never talked about Alice; not just to the woman, to anyone. Until this morning the woman didn't even know Alice existed.

Well, that couldn't have been for very long, could it? Alice says. Now in turn it is she trying to free her hand.

I'm sorry? the woman says icily. She drops Alice's hand like a dead mouse. The sudden lack of resistance sways Alice back.

You said 'since we met', Alice reminds the woman, trying to regain the balance. That couldn't have been that long ago, right?

Adam shoots Alice an outraged look. He no longer sees a reason for her presence here. Inviting her to the Estate was a mistake that he made driven by fear. That morning when he found the new computer shredded to pieces, the knife on the floor, the woman's madness suddenly threatened his own wellbeing. For the first time he questioned his own reasoning; has he really made a mistake living with a stranger? He invited the woman to move in with him so that he could maintain the life that he used to have.

Maybe he also wanted to show that there is someone else. Someone else who's watching out for him; just in case. But what he didn't want was for Alice to chase the woman away.

Let's step inside, shall we? he says with a forced smile.

LIV

Alice laughs out loud; too loud. She's all like this: too much. Overdressed, overscented, overprepared. Like all the people who feel they are not enough, Alice has been trained to overcompensate.

It's not the noise that bothers Liv; sleep deprivation feels like walking around wearing earplugs. From where Liv stands watching, the door between the living room and the kitchen, she can hardly even hear a sound.

But it's Alice's gestures while laughing, her facial expressions, the shaking of her head, that feel excessive. She throws herself around the couch like a fish taken out of water. And like a fish she gasps in-between laughing, making sure she re-fuels the oxygen to keep her going. It's a performance for Adam, magnified by wine and the excitement of their unexpected proximity.

Adam. The man who invited Alice to come here and have

a look at that strange creature he has caught. As if Liv were an exotic bird, a wild animal that he found and took home. At first he couldn't believe his own luck; and so he kept her secret. But then he started realising that the creature he had taken in might not be a pet after all. He decided to maintain a safe distance but held onto her nevertheless. Why? Liv hasn't figured out the exact answer just yet. She senses it must be more than sentiment; that the benefits from having her here are tangible.

But whatever the mysterious profits he has been reaping from her presence, they now seem undermined by her latest behaviour. Hence the invitation. Adam likes to think that he's being cautious. This is a man's way of saying he is scared; terrified even.

The purpose of Alice's inspection is to review Liv's potential for danger. She is here to help tame Liv; disarm her if needed. It must be done tactically; Liv knows that Adam doesn't want her gone. But he needs a witness, an accomplice. Someone who can stay reasonable when he feels he might be losing his mind.

But Alice's presence here violates the silent pact that they made the first night when they ran into each other; the pact of mutual vulnerability, mutual trust. To arm up with Alice is to destabilise the power dynamics. Adam and Liv met as two broken strangers whose paths unexpectedly crossed. Now he is trying to turn her into the other.

Liv knows that he doesn't realise his self-defence is really an attack on her. It's easier to dismiss his own weakness; forget that their rapport was based on mutual frailty. Adam probably tells himself that all he wants is to make her real. But he tries to make her harmless instead. Then he can enslave her, day by day moulding her into becoming Helen.

It's time for Liv to go. No longer a phantom in his mind, she will leave Adam with that small victory. She was seen; she was made real. He couldn't hold on to her, true. But no one could've held on to her, Alice will reassure him. That's just the way with wild creatures: they show up at your door wounded, hurt, in need of shelter and care. You take them in, feed and nurture. But the day they become strong again, you wake up to see that they're gone. Adam will listen to her, nod. Then he will sulk, searching his memory for moments that led her to leave. Every time he finds such a scene, he will film different takes until he discovers how he could've played it to make her stay. She wasn't even worth keeping, Alice will then say, watching his silent agony. It will make Adam angry at first; such a relief to replace sadness with rage. He will direct it at Alice; she won't mind, she'll be happy finally to be put to use. He will defend Liv at first; defend his choice. But then his mind will start recalling those memories that first suggest, but then shout in his face that Alice was right. Liv wasn't even worth keeping.

They will be fine, they will make it work again.

Liv takes another look before she departs. Alice and Adam sit on the sofa; Liv's sofa. Adam makes sure he maintains the distance between them, while Alice relentlessly tries to shorten it. He lets her. He doesn't reciprocate her desire, but encourages it nevertheless. Liv doesn't judge him. She knows that there is both a pleasure and a safety in being wanted so completely. If anyone should understand, it would be her.

Alice leans backward, catching her breath after yet another outburst of laughter. She half-turns to Adam. She has a come-hither look in her eyes which Adam recognises. He smiles, making sure it's just a second too long; just enough to confuse her without a clear promise of ever taking things further. Then he abruptly turns his eyes away, topping their glasses with wine. Everybody plays the same game, Liv realises. It's just that the players assume different positions. She sees Alice's hunger, her urge to satisfy it.

It fascinates Liv to watch him in this new role; the role

she has been accustomed to playing, the one she's assumed with him. It's got a glamorous name: the object of desire. But it means you're nothing else than a parasite, living off someone's love for you. Liv knows; she's always been cast in this part. But there is a trick; the unreciprocated love they have for you doesn't feed you, cannot sustain you. With time, it poisons you. Instead of growing, you wither. And it is them, the disregarded, the rejected, who begin to shine while you are fading away. At first you don't understand; you fool yourself that it is your light they are stealing. But love transforms you into an autotroph; you become your own source of energy.

That's why she did it to Robert, she understands now. It was part envy, part vengeance. She couldn't stand that his love for her became a strength, not a weakness. Every day he woke up with a purpose; exhilarated to find her by his side. It angered her; that joy he sourced from her presence. It didn't feel fair; she thought she was giving him something that she couldn't give herself. Later she told herself he was taking it away from her, and that's why there wasn't enough left. And one day she found the solution which was to finally bring back the balance: if she was the love of his life, then he was to become the story of hers.

We need more wine, Alice exclaims after pouring the last drops into her glass. Liv turns away rapidly. If she wants to leave, she must do it now.

She paces to the hallway, grabs Adam's coat and her purse, puts on her trainers.

Let's move on to some proper drinks. But all three of us, she hears Adam saying. He makes sure to speak loudly, he wants Liv to hear and show up, like a dog trained in obeying the wishes of its owner.

Liv steps out of the door, paces across the corridor. She calls the elevator; she senses that tonight it will prove generous. The building can't wait to spit her out; to have

Adam back all for itself.

She's right. The elevator opens seamlessly. It's that easy, she thinks, stepping inside.

Helen!! she hears Adam's cry resonating across the hallway as the door closes.

A dreadful thought enters her mind. Has she just harmed Adam, the way she had harmed Robert? But then Liv realises she's no runaway in this story; not a real one. She's only stepped in to fill the void after Helen. She's not even a replacement; she's a sub. She, Liv, was never really here.

MARO

He hasn't heard that type of music in years; not in this way. Music listened to for pleasure, gentle. The sounds that daily pour through his headphones serve a different function; they're there to fire him up, prepare for a battle. Staying awake puts you at war with your body. And so martial music has become Maro's permanent companion.

But not tonight. Tonight makes the struggle fade. It is a night of truce; a carnival. They all wear the masks of recreation; rest. Their features become gentle, their smiles delicate, their behaviour almost childlike. And so the soundtrack, too, must change. The soft, chill-out music drips from the walls like a syrup; sugary and thick. It's Titus's latest work, and the primary reason for their celebration. The album received some sort of award, Maro was told. It's a big deal, apparently, and so Thea insisted they must have a party.

Not that the honours from the world have any bearing on one's status here. The Estate knows only two categories: the normal residents and the nocturnal ones. The rights and duties of each group are distinct and do not overlap. But sometimes it feels good to pretend otherwise. Maro understands. He, too, finds a temporary refuge in a masquerade.

And Thea is a mastermind of charades; a high priestess. Her entire life is built upon keeping up appearances, and she has turned them into a solid foundation. Over the years Maro was the only one who managed to uncover her secret. And even he won't call her bluff. Watching Thea run the show is too enjoyable to have it end.

In return, she never disappoints. Tonight she organised the whole buffet with a variety of food and colourful drinks. As if they could still feast, still care about indulging their senses. There are drugs, too, and for the same reason; to let them remember who they used to be. The whole scene is a tribute to their past; there is little in their present in which they could revel. Long gone are the days when their bodies responded to substances. Whatever it is that doesn't let them rest, it never stops, never goes away.

Maro's case, of course, is different. He needs all the discipline and determination to be like them; awake. But they don't know, don't need to.

The light in the underground remains dim, just like any other night. But its source is different: a line of fig scented candles that Thea placed along the edges of the pool. The smell blends with the cigarette smoke, making the air fragrant and heavy. Maro inhales deeply; it tastes like a perfumed pipe tobacco.

Thea brought her paintings, too, turning their cave into a jungle. Maro looks around, thinking how telling that all her works portray wilderness, while all her days are spent here, at the Estate. The things we do for love.

Maro shakes his head in disbelief, and laughs. The laughter is intended as a sincere expression of amusement; that's how Maro views his feelings regarding Thea's relentless efforts. But the sound that comes out of him is more of a snigger, bitter and full of contempt. He halts, alarmed by this new reaction that Thea's situation unexpectedly has triggered.

He's always had nothing but high regard for people's strength, no matter what it is that activates it. Where from then this half-angered, half-sorry response to her predicament? He diagnoses his emotions as pity, and it worries him. Maro knows too well that feeling sorry for others usually hides violent interior motives. What are his? Maro decides that he must be either terrified of sharing Thea's fate or unconsciously envious of her situation.

To investigate the nature of his feelings, Maro searches the room for Thea. The underground is slightly darker than usual, and it takes Maro a while before he spots her resting on a deckchair. Titus is seated by her side, busy massaging her back and shoulders. His hands run across her body with tenderness, and the massage is topped with ever so gentle kisses placed on her skin.

Maro snorts. He cannot help himself; the irrational fury pushes against his skin, needing to explode. Ashamed, he quickly looks to Thea. He wants to find something that would justify his disdain. He searches her face for traces of regret, hollowness. Surely, she must have run empty by now; cannot be sustained by these scraps of affection alone. But despite the unavoidable exhaustion, Thea seems wholesome; radiant even.

Maro turns away, both insulted and frightened by her contentment. And he knows now that it's a combination of terror and envy that prompted his reaction. Two parts of him, which he kept dormant throughout all these years, have awoken. One that knows the costs of love, and the other that is willing to pay the price nevertheless.

Maro looks around, to the others, as to calm himself down. Nobody else here would understand the turmoil that rages now inside of him. Thea's an exception. And so is Maro, it seems.

He turns to the pool. Natasha and Luca are inside, kissing. But Maro knows it's just a pastime, and not an expression of lust or affection. They could've just as well played water volleyball.

Maro looks away, scanning the room for the others. He sees Anna sitting alone at the table, consumed by the chessboard in front of her. She's just set it up, prepared to play against herself. It's a good way to train one's concentration; run through different strategies. Maro, too, is fond of solo chess; he finds it akin to the practice of contemplation. It stimulates the mind while exercising patience. But not tonight, Anna, Maro thinks. I'm afraid tonight you will have to accept a slight change of plans. After all, we are here to party.

Maro stands up. He walks up to the table, aware of the attention that his movements attract. It's nothing new. Maro's like the underground's barometer, and so they all watch him to keep up with any changes.

Now they stop whatever it is that they were doing, busy following his steps. Maro sits by the table. He runs his fingers against the row of pawns and winks at Anna.

Tonight you will have to try anticipating my moves, he says. Not just your own. Anna shrugs her shoulders but Maro can see she's pleased. Sergei appears as if out of nowhere and makes himself comfortable on the side. He dives into his pockets and takes out a few notes. He waves them in the air, making sure everybody notices. He is ready to accept the bets.

Natasha and Luca rush out of the swimming pool. They have no money on them, but Sergei is willing to extend a credit. Natasha bets on Maro, and leans over him. She's convinced she's anyone's lucky charm. Luca has no choice but to back Anna.

Thea and Titus are the last to join. From the corner of his eye Maro sees them rising up unhurriedly, and then moving closer to the game. On the way Thea collects a bottle of whisky and plants it in the middle of the table. They might not drink it, but it sure looks good. Then a terrible tune explodes in the room, rivalling the mellow soundtrack. Maro cringes and looks in the direction the noise comes from.

Alex sits by the pool and strums his guitar. He must have just come in. The last time Maro looked only Natasha and Luca were there. Where the hell did he get a guitar?

No, no, no, Maro mumbles. It's terrible!

What are you talking about? Anna looks up at Maro with confusion. I haven't even made my move yet!

Oh. Not you. Him, Maro raises his head and points to the pool. Alex! he says louder.

But Alex seems not to hear him, deafened by the noise he makes.

Maro used to play the guitar; he used to be a pro. Nobody here would guess, but in his life before the Estate he wrote songs; hits that still resound in the world outside the gate. He knows they've remained popular; it is the royalties that make his current life possible.

Maro grabs the bottle of whiskey and gulps it down
. It fires up his throat, and right then his stomach and his head. After years of strict abstinence it must be a shock to his body; and soon the alcohol will put it in a state of emergency.

I'll be right back, he says to Anna, standing up.

He grabs the bottle and begins walking towards the pool.

Alex! he shouts in the man's direction. Let me show you how it's done.

ADAM

Alice rummages through the kitchen like she is investigating a crime scene. She opens the cupboards, scans the shelves, runs her fingers against the empty surfaces. She performs each action in slow motion; partly due to the amount of alcohol she has consumed and partly to make the whole scene more dramatic. Adam would've never suspected Alice to be the theatrical type.

He watches her with a sense of culpability; none of it would've ever happened if it wasn't for the series of absurd choices that he made. As if taking the woman in wasn't enough, he now had to invite Alice. Like they could zero each other out. It's a mistake gamblers make, a hope the second time will see the luck turn. But Adam is not a gambler; he's never been interested in games of chance. They require a sense of entitlement he lacks. He cannot see why good things are supposed to happen to him; they never have.

So maybe that's just it. Maybe the trigger behind all his choices is not hope but resignation. He never felt he had a right to claim what he truly wanted: Helen. And so he must now submit to what's available: the woman's presence, Alice's love.

Alice pauses by the sink. Whatever it is that she sees, it appears to hold the promise of providing her with clues she was convinced she'd find. She leans forward and picks up a used glass from the sink. Even from a distance Adam sees the lipstick mark. Alice brings the glass closer to her face, examining it carefully. There is a bit of liquid at the bottom. She smells the glass; snorts.

Seems she at least managed to down a drink or two before leaving, Alice says sarcastically.

They look at each other; Alice grins. With triumph; at last she's been proven right. Adam was a fool to take a stranger in, and now he's learned the lesson. The woman not only abandoned him, but exploited his desire to love again.

She didn't 'leave', Adam says angrily. He crosses the kitchen and takes the glass out of Alice's hand.

So where is she? Alice says. She's drunk, he can see it now. If she was sober, she would've known better than to use this moment of Adam's weakness to her advantage. She would've seen that insisting on this victory only pushes him further away. He now finds himself wanting to take the side of the woman. To excuse her earlier behaviour; defend her right to disappear. If anyone was fooled, if anyone could have felt exploited, it would have been her, not Adam.

He also desperately wants her back.

I don't know, he barks. He turns his back to Alice and begins cleaning up the surfaces. Alice's gaze pierces through his shirt. Adam knows she can see she's unexpectedly lost the battle; she doesn't understand how it happened, but she knows it has. He wouldn't have to say another word if he wanted her to leave. All he would need to do was to continue cleaning up the kitchen, while ignoring her presence. After a while she'd say 'I guess I better go then'. She would pause, waiting for him to stop her. She would still see herself as useful: she could help him find the woman, and if they failed, she'd be here to keep him company. Now she'd be the gambler, for some reason hoping for a change of fortune. But she also wouldn't be all that surprised if instead he simply answered 'I'll see you tomorrow' without even turning his back. She'd see herself to the door. And just like that, she'd be gone.

But Adam does turn around. He places his hands on the edge of the bench, leans back. It's a reflex, but the moment his body faces Alice he understands. He must stay in the Estate, and he cannot stay here alone. If it can't be Helen, let it be the woman; if it can't be the woman, let it be anyone. Even Alice.

All I know is that she didn't... she wouldn't leave, he says weakly. He means to sound fragile; it's a confession, and he wants to make sure Alice knows that. Not like this... without a word, he adds, locking his eyes with Alice.

For a moment neither says anything. He can hear Alice's breath speeding up; becoming more shallow. He sees how much this sudden return of intimacy thrills her. But their dynamics have been changing so quickly that she now finds it hard to keep up. She already misunderstood his expectations before; she must tread more carefully this time around.

Maybe she wanted to take a walk or something... Alice says slowly, watching the effect her words have on him. She tests this different approach like a soldier reconnoitring a dangerous terrain. Aware she might get shot; that a wrong step can cause an explosion.

In the middle of the night? Adam says without breaking eye contact. He looks at her helplessly. Alice sighs with relief; she seems to at last understand that it is reassurance that's been expected from her all along. He, too, feels more comfortable playing the antagonist. No longer having to remain collected; having to side with yet another woman who's left him.

Can we call someone? Alice asks. It's a step in the same direction that has proven right only a minute ago. She's trying to come up with a solution; she wants to bring the woman back to Adam, in spite of her own feelings. But what her question has revealed makes Adam sick.

There's no one we can call, he says with a panic in his eyes. I don't know anyone she knows and no one I know knows her. Or of her, he adds.

And you don't even know her real name, right? Alice asks. But it is clear to both of them she doesn't expect an answer. And if she did, he could not give her one.

Adam throws a glass against the wall. The glass shatters. He crouches on the floor. Alice hurries to clean the glass, but Adam stops her. He doesn't want to clean the mess; not yet. First he wants to take a good look at the damage.

LIV

Running through the Estate's corridors feels like she is on a moving walkway. It's not just that there are none of the usual obstacles that used to make Liv mind her every step inside the building; the recurrent falls on the seemingly even floor, the slippery stairs, the collapsing banisters and unattached door handles. It's the push that Liv feels behind her back, like she was in the river, floating with its current. As if the Estate wants to help bring her closer to the exit.

But she cannot be sure. As long as she looks straight ahead, she is convinced the ground is fluctuating. But the moment she looks down, the floor turns still. Maybe the building doesn't want to be caught in the act of advancing Liv's escape. That's fine, she has never been fond of proving one's point. As long as she manages to get out, she is willing to accept that the mysterious workings of the building have been nothing more than a product of her imagination.

She gets to the entrance in record time. The front door opens up widely; never before has she noticed that the door is automated. But just as she steps forward, about to go back to the world she had fled, a familiar sound draws her head to the side.

The vibration is very gentle, and weakens even more as it travels through the air to reach Liv's ears. And yet she recognises it, the way she would if she heard her own name. Turning her head is then an impulse, and falls outside the category of making a decision. She doesn't choose to halt and turn; it simply happens.

But it's not a name that Liv hears, not even a word. It's a splash; a loud splash of water, which resonates across the hallway, bouncing off the walls.

She turns away from the entrance and walks towards the source of the sound. It comes from behind the door which has been left ajar; the door to the underground.

Liv's movements are now extremely slow. Like she is walking against the stream, submerged in a muddy, dense fluid that impedes her movements.

But she doesn't mind the obstruction; she almost enjoys the resistance that her body must fight. Whatever awaits her behind the door, she prefers to approach it unhurriedly.

Liv feels like she is in a trance, hypnotised by the recurrent sounds of water. With every step she takes the sounds vibrate with greater resonance. She is sure now that she has heard it before; she has heard it every night since she has moved in here. It is this melody that has kept her awake.

MARO

Maro recognises the melody; it's Springsteen's Atlantic City. And it's being slaughtered.

He picks up the pace. The quicker he gets to the pool, the quicker he can intervene. But as he moves, the tune penetrates through his clothes and skin, weakening the seal blocking his memories. Once loosened, the archive of his past experience ruptures like a cyst. Maro feels sick. As if the pus from the buried, festering wounds is now running freely through his circulatory system; poisoning him.

It is hard to believe that even such profane execution by someone lacking any skill fails to strip the music of its power to transport across time and space. It ships Maro not only to a different place and a different era, but to a different body. A body that slept; loved. And he is forced to feel exactly what the other had felt then. But without the scaffolding that had held him together in the past, he collapses.

It is his fall that makes the music stop. And without the soundtrack, the memories vanish. As if someone unplugged a projector which was screening a series of slides. Silence and void, an all-encompassing hollowness, follow shortly after. Maro revels in this reclaimed peace; at last he lets go of his usual vigilance. And he falls asleep.

Not for long; no longer than the scheduled naps that he takes daily. But it is the depth of his sleep that terrifies Maro once he wakes up. As if he was underwater, he now struggles to breathe.

What's wrong?! Alex shouts. He holds Maro's arms in an attempt to lift him up. But Maro's body is too large, too heavy. It resists being moved, and so Alex settles for a squeeze; it gives him an illusion he's helping.

Everything, Maro whispers. But with candour, not sarcasm. The response surprises both of them. It reveals a greater panic than he had intended; sounds more alarming than he was willing to admit; even to himself.

What do you mean? Alex asks with caution. Maro knows that this sudden confession troubles Alex. Everyone here carries a heavy burden; their collective rapport is built on a dismissal of the lives that exist outside the underground. They come here every night to remember what it means to live; not just make it through the days, wrestling with every hour. This place is a substitute of sleep; not quite the same, but it lets them disconnect. Reset, recharge. Not much, but just enough to face another day.

No wonder Alex now treads carefully, reluctant to accept the approaching calamity. He knows he'd become the collateral damage of whatever is shaking the foundations of Maro's life.

But Maro won't do it; not to Alex. He points to the guitar instead, which lays abandoned on the edge of the pool. Maro frowns, exaggerating his displeasure.

That bad? Alex laughs. It's a hearty laughter; a sincere expression of joy triggered by Maro's retreat. Whatever happened a few minutes ago, they manage to push it away, protect their safe space here.

You have no idea, Maro says. He notices that the bottle of whiskey, which he dropped when falling, didn't break. He picks it up; there is still a bit of liquor left at the bottom. Maro takes a long sip, finishes it. He cleans his mouth with the outside of his hands. But worry not, he says, grinning. Here I am, ready to show you how it's done.

Alex stands up, laughing. He throws his hands up, defeated. He doesn't mind Maro showing him how it's done.

Alex turns around, about to get the guitar. But as he approaches the pool, he sees something that makes him freeze. Maro cannot tell what it is; Alex's back restricts Maro's view. It must be someone at the door; Alex stands facing the entrance. Someone new, Maro thinks; the adrenaline rush speeds up his heart rate, his breath.

He stands up to see for himself. His body is still weak from the collapse and he struggles to keep his balance. But once he's back on his feet, he doesn't look at the door; not yet. Let it be her, he prays in his mind. But he still doesn't look. He needs more time to prepare himself.

Only when he's ready he follows Alex's gaze. And immediately meets Liv's eyes, watching him. She's always one step ahead; always the first to see.

Maro smiles, and his smile is a rope which he throws at her, in desperate hope that she will catch the other end. But something goes wrong; he might've forgotten how the smiles that tie up two people across a room or a street, making the surroundings fade, work. It's been so long since he's smiled like this.

Instead of recognition, it is panic that takes over Liv's face. It's only a flash, like lightning. And then she's gone.

Alex jumps up towards the entrance, in an instant regaining the control over his body.

Don't! Maro shouts. Alex slows down. But he keeps moving towards the door despite Maro's protest.

Let her go, Maro barks. It's an order, not a request; they both know it. Alex has no choice but to stop. He turns around to face Maro.

He's furious now and doesn't try to hide it. On the contrary, he wants Maro to know. Alex doesn't understand what just happened; and he dislikes being reminded of the hierarchy here. The division of power in the Estate is very subtle, barely noticeable. When everything runs smoothly, everybody simply minds their own business. The building has ways to correct petty misconducts on a daily basis; it's primarily self-regulating. Maybe that's what makes it so difficult to accept whenever one is reminded of the rules. And these are simple; decisions made by the founders. Like Maro. But also like Adam.

But she might... Alex objects.

She won't, Maro says firmly. He knows he's right. He also knows this is a point of no return. That feeling he had earlier tonight was a warning. A gut instinct, always few steps ahead of him.

How can you be so sure? Alex asks, watching Maro carefully. Alex senses something is not quite right; smells trouble ahead.

Trust me, Maro says. She'll be back.

ADAM

One moment Alice's hand runs through his hair, the other it bounces off his head as if it touched something hot.

You're back! she shouts.

Adam freezes. He doesn't have to turn around to know; the woman is back. He sits still, feeling the woman's gaze drill a hole in his skull. Her eyes then move down, like a laser cutting across his neck, moving down his shoulders; his back. It burns his skin, which melts under the heat and opens him up. Shame spills out of Adam's entrails; it spreads across the sofa, across the floor. It carries a terrible stench.

He closes his eyes, cringing with revulsion. Why did he let Alice touch him? He dreaded the idea of her hands in close proximity to his skin, and yet did nothing to stop her. But maybe it was the idea of her touch that appalled him, and not the touch itself. Maybe he just wanted to be caressed, to feel the fingers of a woman run through his hair, stroke his face. And what he dreaded was to be caught in the act, and not the act itself. To be seen suckling the scraps of affection; to become someone who feeds off trash.

Of course I'm back, why wouldn't I be? the woman says coolly.

Adam jumps up in his seat. She's seen him, his disgrace, and she didn't leave. She's not only back; she's here to stay. For now, the fear whispers. But Adam silences it. He collects himself; sucks up his spilled shame like a vacuum; zips himself up. Back in one piece, he turns to face the woman.

She still has her coat; the coat in which she arrived here. It looks ominous, as if she could still change her mind; take off at any moment.

Adam paces towards her to remove it. He resolves to get rid of it the following day. He will buy her a new coat; any coat she wishes.

We were so worried! he says to the woman. You've been gone for hours.

She looks at him then; and it's the first time in weeks that her eyes are so alert. Weeks ago, she had entered the Estate as one person; tonight she had left his flat as another. And now she returns as someone else altogether. But not someone new; on the contrary, it's the first time Helen truly perforates through the woman's skin; her eyes. The woman and Helen superimposed is the person who now stands in front of him. And Adam knows in an instant; she had found them.

He takes her in his arms to hide his thrill, and his terror. She lets him.

I wanted to get a bit of fresh air, she says. Her voice is gentle, with undertones of amusement. As if she just found herself a new game she can play.

From the moment she returns, she makes sure to address only Adam, as if Alice wasn't there.

I must have lost track of time, the woman adds, bending forward to kiss Adam on the lips.

For nearly two hours? Alice says with fury, pointing to her phone.

The woman does not turn to Alice but pulls away from Adam.

I really don't understand why I am suddenly being interrogated in my own house, she says to Adam.

Adam's, Alice barks.

The woman finally turns to Alice. It's a slow half-turn; a regal gesture, aimed to stress her response is based on her kindness, despite the unworthiness of the person she is about to address.

Sorry? she says.

Adam's house, Alice barks.

That's enough, Alice, he says. Adam doesn't raise his voice, but his tone is sharp.

Seriously?! Alice at last loses her cool.

It's probably better if we call it a night, he says, pointing to the door. We're all a little tired.

Alice bridles at this injustice, but says nothing. Instead, she storms towards the door. She turns at the last moment, just before stepping out. Before she speaks, she makes sure to catch Adam's eyes; lock them.

Can't believe you let her get away with this... Alice hisses.

LIV

The temperature in the apartment is optimal; that is noticeable. It's the first morning here that Liv is neither trembling nor sweating. She opens her eyes. It's a habit; even if she cannot sleep, she still spends the end of the night lying still, her eyes shut.

Once she opens up her eyes, she finds the light, just like the temperature, perfect. It brightens the room without blinding her. At last Liv gets to start the day without fighting her environment; without having to push against the hostility that would normally vibrate from the walls.

She stretches across the sofa, unexpectedly rested. That's also new; that feeling of complete relaxation. She still hasn't slept; she knows that won't change. But she is no longer worried. She has found the source.

Because that's how she sees the underground; as a charger that she's been missing ever since she moved in with Adam. From now on every night she'll be able to plug in; revitalise.

She'll stay here then, in the Estate. Where else did she think she was going anyway? The truth is she wasn't thinking about it; she never had. It's just something she does; whenever in danger, she runs. Liv's a runaway who has run out of places to hide.

But now she will stay here, among people who are just like her. At first she must stay with Adam; he'll let her. Liv still doesn't understand what it is that glues him to her, but watching him with Alice confirmed her earlier instinct. She's not only perfectly replaceable; she, Liv, has never really been here. Adam needs a woman and that's what she has been; a woman. This impersonal status takes away the guilt, the responsibility; each of them looks after oneself. It also makes Liv feel more at ease, freer; knowing that she's not trapped here, that the situation is both tentative and easy to amend.

She jumps on her feet, transformed by the events of last night, but also by her resolve to stay. Renewal spreads across her body. She's famished. Now she remembers that she hasn't had a proper meal for weeks. But never during these weeks has she felt hungry; sleeplessness took her appetite away. It must be that shot of energy she's just received; it demands fuel.

But to eat, she needs to get out of the Estate, and go back

to the world. There is no real food in the house; other than some old bread, cereal and coffee. Adam eats at work while Liv hardly ever feels hungry. Or she hasn't, until now.

The thought of having to step outside the gate doesn't bother her. On the contrary, for the first time since she's arrived here, Liv finds the idea of a field trip quite appealing. She feels ready to venture back to the world for a few hours. More than ready; she feels obliged to leave the Estate; to let it rest.

Liv walks to the front door. She puts her trainers on and is about to grab her coat, but all she sees inside the closet is a hanger. Her coat is gone.

She feels the adrenaline rush across her body. There is a part of her that knows already. And the other one that silences it; doesn't even want to hear that possibility being put into words.

Liv walks up to the door, presses the handle. The door is closed. She presses it again, a bit harder, then pushes the door. Nothing.

Adam never locks the door when he leaves her inside; Liv knows he wouldn't have forgotten. Her keys were in the coat that he must have taken. And left, closing her inside the apartment.

RUNAWAYS

MARO

Maro watches the ice cubes melt. He's placed the bag on his lap; the warmth of his skin carries through the fabric of his trousers, through the plastic that wraps the ice. It raises the temperature, defrosting the cubes. Why isn't it the other way around, Maro ponders. Where from such vitality in his body, such insistence to fight? Couldn't the cold of the ice travel through the plastic, the fabric, until it reached his skin? And then freeze it, turning him into a statue. Or a large snowman, sitting on the bench. But no. Surprisingly, his body is still alive; so alive in fact that it defeats the ice.

It also begins to cool down. The body transferred the energy to heat up the ice, lowering its own temperature. Where his body continues finding the energy, Maro can't tell. But either way, he's succeeded; it is the cold that helps him stay awake. And ever since last night, he feels like he's on fire.

He dives his hand into the bag. He feels nothing, or very little. Not cold or pain; rather, he senses a change of matter. His hand inside the bag turns the solid particles into water. He holds it there for a twelve seconds. When he takes it out, the skin is very red.

Maro now puts his other hand inside the bag and fishes out one of the few remaining cubes. He holds it in his fingers; moves towards his mouth. In the last moment Maro changes direction; instead of putting the cube into his mouth, he touches his cheek. He runs the ice cube across his exhausted, puffy face.

And yet again, his skin begins melting it. When the cube disappears, he is about to reach for another but changes his mind. He shakes the bag and then bends over, dipping his whole face in the icy water with tiny crystals floating on its surface. When he pulls his head out, even these disappear. Yet again, his body proved destructive and indestructible.

LIV

Liv's hand freezes just an inch from the wall. She was about to hit it, to punch it until she grows weak again; until she uses up all this pathetic energy she's woken up with. As if she was in the hands of a sadist; her wish was granted precisely when it had become perfectly worthless. But she knows that this time it's not the building's work; it's Adam's. He locked her in here. And so there is no point in hurting the wall; it won't break. It is her own hand that might. And she needs to keep herself intact if she wants ever to get out of this apartment. Instead, she wishes to smash Adam's head against the wall; imagines the sound of his skull crushing. She's fuming.

But she doesn't feel hopeless, the way she used to feel when it was her against the building; that battle couldn't have been won. Then she was truly trapped. Fighting against Adam is easier, especially since she feels the silent support of the Estate. Even now, it feels as if the walls oozed a cold breeze that soothes Liv's fury; calms down her breath. She's one of the residents now, one of the nocturnals; she belongs here. And so she's not alone in her struggle, she will be saved.

Liv turns away from the wall; she walks up to the window. Her face brightens up; Maro. He sits in his usual spot; the bench. But his face is buried in a large bag that he holds on his lap. Liv knocks on the window.

Maro! she shouts.

Maro remains bent forward, motionless. The sounds from the apartment seem not to reach him. Liv bangs on the glass, but he still doesn't move; doesn't hear her. She pulls back; the despair slowly begins to take over. Just as she bites her lips to stop herself from weeping; a gust of wind blows on her neck. She trembles; then freezes. It can't be; the windows don't open. But there it is again; the wind. She stretches out her arm and gently presses the glass surface. The fixed frame window opens with ease.

ADAM

The desk is cluttered; chaotic. It fascinates Adam how quickly the mess accumulates, gets out of control. He watches it grow, wants to see where it stops; whether it stops at all.

When he arrived in the office earlier today everything was as usual; spotless. Then he took out of his pocket the extra set of keys that the woman would use. He had to; it was burning a hole in his pocket, making him unable to concentrate. The keys caught on an old receipt and for some reason, he didn't feel like removing it. It went from there: a hand-out from the briefing, some post that just got delivered, half-empty coffee cups, scratch notes. Whoever comes by his office automatically adds something to the pile; Adam's left with a range of pens and papers that do not belong to him.

Now in the middle of this hoard lands a laptop. Adam doesn't immediately look up; for a while he just marvels at how perfectly it crowns the state of his desk. The pencil underneath makes the laptop wobble, signalling it might fall at any given moment. Clever, he thinks.

I knew it! he hears Alice's voice crying out just above his head.

Adam likes how her laptop fits into today's theme. But he has no interest in looking at the screen, finding out whatever it is that made her storm into his office like this.

He wouldn't have minded if she'd left it here: it serves a decorative function, almost a symbolic function. But he knows it would be too much to ask, even for him, even of someone like Alice. He has no choice but to lift up the computer and hand it back to her.

I'm hours behind, Alice, he says as a way of explaining. Whatever it is, I'm sure it can wait, he adds.

Adam smiles politely and looks down. He pulls out one of the random papers lying on the desk and matches it with a golden pencil; who knew - at times even mess can prove useful. The paper is already covered in somebody else's calculations, so Adam simply starts adding up new numbers; there is no way Alice can know it's all meaningless scribbles. His work, whatever it might be, would normally be reason enough for her to exit quietly, not counting the apology

But not this time. Alice doesn't even make an attempt to move. Instead, she leans forward, watching him closely.

You must be the last person in the world who still does it the old way, she says with such fondness that Adam doesn't have to look up to know she's smiling.

His hand halts, as if paralysed by this relentless, misdirected affection.

Don't get me wrong, she adds quickly. I love it.

Poor Alice, misreading him as usual. Something in Adam breaks; he knows too well the agony of the incessant dance around someone whose good grace conditions your own existence. And so he looks up, forces not just a smile, but a smile that smuggles traces of warmth, care.

I'm sorry again about last night, he says. I didn't mean to...to... Adam stutters. What is it exactly that he apologises to her for? Use you, he should say. I'm sorry I used you. I didn't mean for things to get out of hand.

It would be closest to the truth. But he can't say that.

Kick me out? Alice comes to his assistance, laughing. Clearly his willingness to make amends is enough.

That's fine, she says quickly. Or it will be, if you just have a quick look at this.

Alice gently pushes the computer back towards Adam. He sighs but cannot say no now.

What is it? Adam asks, looking at the screen. It's a news site; one of the main ones, if he remembers correctly. He stopped following any news once he moved into the Estate;

the matters of the outside world have no bearing on the residents.

Before Adam looks away, he automatically registers the title 'The Mystery Behind the Missing Author'.

Or who is it, you might want to ask, Alice says. Have a look.

Adam looks back to the screen. He now notices the picture below the title; a picture of a woman. He looks closer; it looks like a picture of the woman. Adam freezes; it can't be. He brings the computer closer, unable to look away.

She looks like...like... Helen...

More like Liv, Alice says. Liv Campbell, the bestselling missing author of creative non-fiction, or however they call it. I knew her face looked familiar!

I've never heard of her... Adam says, trying to read the article.

Name an author you've heard of, Alice snorts. A living author.

Actually, he knows a couple of writers. He knows them personally; he's never read a line written by any of them. Letters have never been his thing; he's always preferred numbers.

One whose accounts you're not handling, Alice narrows down her challenge.

Fair point, Adam thinks. He shrugs and looks back at the screen. He reads for a few seconds.

It says here that her boyfriend died in some mysterious circumstances... Adam says, turning back to Alice. Just before the release of her latest book.

Or more likely killed himself, she says. The bitch was writing about him.

MARO

Maro's head hurts from the noise. But today it's not the

music; the headphones, hanging around his neck, are muted. The sounds he hears form words; he can discern whole sentences. They're at war with each other; it's a verbal Guernica.

Some speak of retribution, punishment. These ones he knows; cherishes. They've fuelled him throughout the years. Not only doesn't he fear them, but he'd like to think that he's authored them. They're his, Maro's.

But not all of the voices that now resound in his head are dreadful. That's not a good thing; he's committed an unforgivable crime. There is no space for messages of love or compassion. They only break his beaten-up heart all over again.

Even worse are the voices that seek excuses, demanding redemption; these appal him more than the part of him that did it. Cowardice has always seemed to Maro worse than violence.

And all of them undermine Maro's version of what happened; unsettle him by planting a seed of doubt.

Maybe that's why he kept the music loud; so as not to hear them. And it wasn't the staying awake that has been the worst of punishments he could conceive of; maybe even worse would be hearing the voices. Maybe it wasn't a punishment at all; maybe it was an escape. If he ever let himself rest, they would seize him. He would have become possessed.

And back then Maro knew straight away that he could not afford uncertainty. Only a severe, perfectly executed punishment could have preserved his sanity. He could count on no one but himself; Maro was in the hands of fools who believed he'd suffered enough. Or maybe that's just something that he was told; and in fact they weren't fools at all but sadists, waiting to see the guilt driving him into madness.

Either way, Maro disobeyed the sentence, or the lack thereof, and found his own way to serve justice. He has maintained lucidity of mind by allowing it to destroy his body. For that, he needed to reinforce a single truth; to stick to one version of what happened. There was no space for polyphony; for all the different voices to express their own truths.

Whose views they represented and where they came from, Maro's never known. But he's always believed that the monistic view of man is an illusion. Each human is like planet Earth; seen from the outside everybody appears to be an entity, but inside there is a multitude of beings, usually at war with each other.

And now Maro's head, too, is once again a battlefield. The silence that surrounds him lets the voices speak. Or maybe they've been speaking all along; it was just too loud for him to hear them. It might've been a trick he's been playing all along; unable to supress the voices, he chose to stun himself.

But it is no longer just about him; Liv needs him. And so he must sober up; facing all the pain that this process entails.

He squats in front of the door; the door to Adam's flat. He runs his hand across the door's lock. It looks spotless; there's not a trace of a break-in. And yet Maro knows that they've broken not just the lock, but the rules of the Estate; the residents cannot intervene in the affairs of private households. No matter what happens, they cannot enter other apartments uninvited. There will be consequences, Maro has no doubt. Transgressions tend to cause a domino effect; one inevitably leads to another. But maybe that's something that must happen; the fall of the old order.

You're good, Maro says, watching the door. He straightens up, turns around. Sergei and Liv stand behind him.

Liv looks frightened, like a wild animal that's just been freed from a trap. She stands with crossed arms, running her hands across her shoulders and neck, as if investigating the damage. Once she makes sure that everything is in the right place, she'll run away again. There's no point in trying to tame her; she needs a reason to stay. Maro knows he doesn't have much time to give her one.

Sergei's posture contrasts with Liv's; his whole body beams with joy. No, more than joy; a sense of accomplishment. It's the first time that Maro sees life shining through Sergei's paper-thin, waxy skin. That's what he excelled in before moving in here; that's what in the end had him banished; breaking and entering. Maro knows little about the specifics of Sergei's crimes, other than that he had little interest in whatever was inside the places he unlocked. He let the others take care of whatever business had waited for them inside. All he was concerned with was removing whatever it was that blocked the entrance.

Old habits die hard, eh? Maro asks.

Sergei, pretending to be annoyed, waves him off and instead turns to Liv.

It's as though you had your own key, he says. No sign of breaking in.

You want to go get your things? Maro asks, gently touching Liv's bare arm. She's in a dress; the very same dress she was wearing the first night he spotted her at the party.

I've got no things, Liv says.

Maro cannot help but quickly run their eyes across Liv's figure. She has no suitcase, no bag, not even a coat to cover her bare shoulders. Only a small purse hanging from her shoulder. So she truly just walked from the party straight to Adam's apartment; never went back wherever she's come from to get her things. Other than the books, and even these she didn't want to keep.

Maro knows that Sergei's doing just the same; he catches a glimpse of him from the corner of his eye. They're both scanning Liv; taken aback by this unexpected discovery.

But who are they to ask questions. Maro notices that Sergei looks away; he's trained in minding his own business.

And so should Maro be. He snaps out of this momentary daze and smiles at her.

So you're ready to go? Maro makes sure.

Liv is about to nod, but she suddenly hesitates. She looks back at the apartment, pauses. When she turns back to them again, Maro knows she's resolved something.

Do you happen to have any nails in your box? she asks Sergei.

Sergei does not show a sign of surprise. He opens the box; dives in. He stretches out an arm in front of Liv. Maro sees how her eyes shine when she sees a bunch of various sized nails; shine with mischief.

Give me one minute! she shouts and runs back to the apartment.

Please, let it really be just a minute, Maro silently prays. He can handle the many voices in his head, if he continues hearing one single voice outside of it; Liv's.

LIV

Liv puts the thickest nail against the wall; hits it with a hammer. It sinks in as if the building was made of butter, not bricks. She's not surprised; she's sensed that after everything that happened she'd be at last allowed to do it; leave a mark. Or more like get to feel as if she wasn't entirely helpless; Liv believes that it's a kind of retribution for Adam's attempts to trap her here. He probably could've done as he wished with his own guest. But last night she became one of them; the residents. And the building takes care of its own.

Liv picks up her failed reproduction of Dali's painting and hangs it on Adam's wall. He took her coat, she'll leave him the painting. She knows he'll hate it; her making changes to the place where Helen lived, becoming anything other than her sub. It disrupts the order; violates the past.

She hangs it upside down, so that the elephants now

reflect the swans.

Now she's ready to leave, even though she knows that the change to Adam's apartment might not be permanent. She's almost certain that when the time is right, the wall will shake off the painting, the nail; and seal the hole. Liv has no illusions about her own agency at the Estate; the power she now possesses is the power she's been given, and which can be taken away at any given moment. But all she wants is for Adam to see the painting on the wall and feel as if he stepped into a landslide; the way he made her feel earlier today. She wants him falling, with no one around to give him a hand to hold. And there is a good chance that the building might want that too.

As she steps out of the apartment, she realises how much everything has changed. When she moved in, she'd planned to leave as if she was never here. But now it's too late for that; Adam violated the terms of their engagement, she had come with nothing but her coat. And he took that away.

She faces the door, places both hands on its surface. She knows that when she pushes it, the door will close; there will be no way of opening it again without asking for Sergei's help.

She turns to Maro and Sergei.

And you say he won't call the police? Liv asks.

Oh honey, Sergei says with a condescending smile. He puts a hand on the door and pushes it. Liv's heart jumps; the door locks.

It's like you were never here, Sergei says.

ADAM

He has never been to a bookstore. Maybe once or twice as a little kid, but he can't be sure, can't remember. He's always lived in the world of numbers rather than letters. But he gets why people would read books; why they would like to escape. People in the world outside the gate, that is. The residents are one step ahead; they have already escaped. The Estate is the final getaway.

He suddenly wonders whether there are any residents who still read. But he can't imagine how anyone would keep books in the Estate; there aren't even any shelves to put them on. If anyone had arrived with books, they probably stored them in boxes. If someone still wants to read after moving into the Estate; they must do so during the day, when they step outside the gate, leaving the Estate behind.

Adam looks around the bookstore, suddenly overwhelmed by the intensity of his own experience. He'd planned to simply head to one of the store assistants and request Liv's book. He'd called in before the visit; the book has been put aside for him. But he didn't anticipate how much he'd like it here.

To his surprise, the place smells great. Adam walks around the shelves, picking up random copies, flipping through the pages. He would have never guessed how many types of paper a book can be printed on. Some smell clean and crisp, like a cologne designed to imitate a breeze. Then others give a warm whiff of wood dried in the sun. There are sleek aromas and coarser ones; the latter itch the inside of his nostrils and throat.

After sniffing them, Adam sneezes a few times, coughs. But then he goes back to inhaling the books; even these with grainier textures. He's always appreciated the difficult scents; they're hardest to forget.

Only after a while Adam realises he's being watched. But not the way he's used to; with care. In the Estate to be watched means to be looked after. But here people point fingers at him, laugh. It reminds Adam how lucky he is to be chosen to live in the Estate. There he has the comfort of being always seen, but never mocked.

He paces to the counter. The man behind the counter picks

up Liv's book; Adam feels the rush of adrenaline. Like he's about to walk inside a room that's been locked before him for weeks. No, more like a room he didn't even know was there; as if he leaned against a wall that suddenly slid open.

The man, who must roughly be the same age as Adam, notices his excitement. He looks again at the cover; raises his eyebrows suggestively, smiles.

Liv Campbell, *A Possible Husband*, he reads. What a book, huh? he asks, looking up at Adam.

Across the counter Adam moves uncomfortably and looks away.

Well, I haven't read it yet, so... Adam says reluctantly. The last thing he needs now are spoilers; he feels that the article that Alice had shown him earlier already revealed too much.

Yeah, sure, the man says, shrugging his shoulder. Me neither, he adds winking at Adam.

Adam looks at him entirely bewildered. Might it be a custom in the bookstores to discuss with customers books that neither party has read? Adam wouldn't know. He hands the man his credit card, hoping to exchange it for the book. But the man takes the card while holding on to the book. He scans it; leans forward.

I more meant the story... he whispers confidentially.

The story? Adam asks, pulling back. The books might smell superb; but the bookstore assistants still smell like humans.

Oh, you know, the man raises his eyebrows suggestively. The story behind the story, ha! he laughs, at last handing Adam the book.

But he doesn't take his eyes off Adam's face, and after a few seconds he clasps his hands in theatrical astonishment. Just as Adam was about to turn away.

No!! Don't tell me you haven't heard of it?! the man cries out.

Heard of what? Adam says, making the dual mistake of encouraging him to talk, but also of not removing the book from the man's sight quickly enough. In an instant the book is again taken by the assistant, who now shakes it in front of Adam's eyes.

Apparently it's all true, the man says. Word for word. Robert...He points to the cover. That is, presumably... The assistant reads the title: *A Possible Husband*. He looks up at Adam. The book's main protagonist... he explains. Adam frowns, expectantly.

Well, he killed himself shortly after reading the manuscript, the assistant cuts to the chase, at last noticing Adam's annoyance. But he still can't resist adding in a personal reflection. Who knows which of the disclosed secrets hurt him most... the man ponders.

Adam's had enough. He reaches out for the book. The man resists for a second, then lets go, shrugging his shoulders with a mixture of disappointment and hurt. He looks back to his screen, but cannot resist finishing off the story.

Anyway, when the news hit the press the book was already in print and heading to the bookstores, there was nothing to be done. But the writer... the man again turns to read from the cover. Liv Campbell...he looks up at Adam. She vanished.

What do you mean 'vanished'? Adam asks. Vanished how?

The man smiles with satisfaction. He slowly takes away the eyes off the screen. He makes sure to lock Adam's eyes first; then he snaps his fingers in front of his face.

Just like that, he says.

MARO

Maro hardly looks like an athlete; maybe a retired one. Or injured. He's got the frame, the posture. But he's too heavy for anyone to believe that he could be fast enough; too lethargic to appear dangerous.

But he follows the daily routine of a competitive sportsman. The relentless training makes his body sore. Maro fills the bathtub with water and ice, walks in. He submerges himself in the cold; the ice flushes lactic acid out of his muscles, reduces swelling. It's not pleasant, not at first. The body fights against him; it doesn't know that the temporary discomfort is exactly what it needs.

Maro can't blame his body for its lack of trust; they share a long history of abuse and exploitation. It must be hard to believe that spending eight minutes in an ice bath is a favour; that it's the least he can do for his over-performing muscles. But to remain an act of kindness, the bath cannot exceed ten minutes; Maro must keep an eye on the time.

After a minute or two, his body slowly gives in, begins to relax. He watches it float on the surface; his knees like little bare islands erupting from the sea of ice. He checks the time; three minutes have gone by, leaving him with five minutes to kill.

He lets himself close his eyes. The space inside him feels motionless. His neurons, just like the blood vessels, seem to have shrunk; he feels nothing. The voices are silent; frozen. The ice transforms his inner war zone into a safe space.

Maro tightens the grip on the rim of the bathtub and lowers himself. He rests the back of his head on ice, letting it submerge in the cold bath. He, too, sinks into the chasm. He's now neither asleep nor fully awake; neither alive nor dead.

He's at home here; underwater, underworld, underground. These are Maro's natural habitats, his realms of existence. They let him hibernate.

LIV

She bends over the bathtub. Maro's body is fully submerged in ice, with only a pair of knees and face sticking out above the surface. She's not worried; he breathes rhythmically, inhaling through the nose and exhaling through the mouth. The warm air forms a cloud, like a speech balloon in a comic.

Liv stretches out her hand. She writes 'Tell me a secret' with her finger in the air. She turns to Maro; just to watch him, but his eyes suddenly open. He looks at her as if he heard her; heard words she didn't even voice.

Liv jumps up, but Maro's quicker; he's already got a hold of her hand. The cold of his grip travels through her own skin. Liv shivers. She jerks her hand, trying to free herself. He releases his clutch, but keeps his hand on her arm.

Liv pushes him away. She turns away and runs towards the exit.

Wait! she hears him scream. It sounds like a command, and to her own surprise, she obeys. She halts; waits for whatever it is that he wants to tell her.

Easy, Maro says. Like she was a horse that's about to run away. She suddenly feels an urge to look at him; to see how he looks looking at her. And so she must turn, and as she turns she realises she's gone too far away to notice the details of his face; she must come closer. She walks a few steps towards the bathtub.

Maro sits up, hugging his knees.

Is that what you do? he asks. Run away?

Yes, Liv thinks, but says nothing. She doesn't have to; he knows.

Maro nods and stands up. Liv immediately looks away. Maro's nudity still makes her embarrassed, even if he doesn't seem to feel any shame. He grabs a towel; begins to unhurriedly dry himself.

That's fine, Maro says. He's referring to her running

away, but the casualness of his voice feels offensive; as if he didn't notice how uncomfortable he made her feel.

That's fine, Liv thinks. She looks back at him. She first makes sure to lock their eyes, and then moves her gaze down, taking her time to investigate every inch of his skin.

She doesn't get very far. Maro quits drying his skin and wraps the towel around his hips instead.

Liv snorts. And now it is Maro who exits the bathroom. He passes Liv without a word. But as he reaches the door, he pauses.

If you really want to run away - do it! he says. But don't run away just because it's something you always do.

He leaves the bathroom the moment he finishes the sentence; leaving her time to think, space to decide. He doesn't want her to respond; not just yet.

Liv hesitates. How is she supposed to know the difference? She's always thought she was made to run. If she ever wanted to stay, would she even know how?

She can't tell; not yet.

For now she needs, wants more time. And time is something that Maro has already offered her, so she decides to accept his offer. It doesn't feel greedy on her part, nor generous on his; if the Estate is abundant in one thing, it's time. That's the main difference between this place and the world outside the gate; everybody here has time.

ADAM

He puts the key in the door; it turns with ease. It's hard to say why it surprises Adam; why there is a part of him that anticipated trouble. Maybe it's the law of retribution; Adam's aware of his own transgression. He knows he locked the woman up against her will; while she was asleep, unable to even put up a fight. He had broken the Estate's code of conduct; the doors here can be locked, but only from the inside. This place is a fortress, not a jail. To overstep the Estate's rules is an error, but to manipulate with its nature is a crime. The consequences are unavoidable, it's simply a matter of time.

Adam pushes the door, walks in.

Helen? he shouts. It's no mistake; he wants once more to hear himself say this name out loud. More than just say; call it, address someone with the genuine hope of being responded to. It's probably the last time he can get away with this. In the course of the day she has transformed from the woman he's taken in into Liv Campbell; she's been named, come to be in her own right. He had thought of her as a sub for Helen, while all along she's been an author, running away from her own story.

Helen?! Adam repeats, this time louder.

There is no response. Adam automatically glances at the hangers; the empty spot where the woman's coat used to be makes his heart stop. It takes a second before Adam remembers that it is he who took her coat away.

He takes out the book from his pocket, studies the cover.

Or shall I call you Liv...? he murmurs.

He puts down his briefcase, straightens up. Just as he is about to walk into the apartment, he freezes with his foot already lifted in the air. It can't be.

Adam gently puts down his foot again; steps back. He bends forward just as when he was when putting down the briefcase. He remains in this position for a while, staring at the gap in a straight row of shoes. The woman's trainers are gone. And unlike the coat, it wasn't he who took them.

Adam remains in this position for a while, letting the dread spill across his body. Only then he sprints ahead, storming into the living room.

Liv!!! Adam cries out.

But there is no sign of the woman; no sign of Liv.

Instead, there is a painting hanging on the wall. Adam

walks up closer. It's the painting that Liv had brought. The only thing she brought with her; the only thing she's left. When Adam saw it for the first time, he had wondered why of all things that she could take with her, she chose a small, abstract canvas of questionable quality. It felt symbolic; she was marking her territory, claiming the space. But Adam wasn't worried; he didn't say a word. He knew that the Estate is no place for conquerors. The bare walls would remain bare, regardless of her efforts.

He now moves his face close to the canvas; his nose almost touching the dried out roughness of paint. The odour of varnish and turpentine has almost evaporated; for most people it would be undetectable at this point. But Adam sniffs the remnants of its aroma as if he was inhaling its soul. As his gaze travels up the painting, he is stricken by an appearance of a third note; a strong scent of fresh concrete, mixed with something else. He halts, closes his eyes, breathes in. It's something musty, as if a smell of mould. He opens his eyes; there is a nailhead right in front of him.

Adam goes pale. He reaches out with shaking hands, taking the painting off the wall. The nail pierces right through the wall; and it is the smell of this wound that Adam has detected. It fascinates him that the walls, less than five years old, are saturated with the odour of its fundaments; the mould must be shooting off from the underground, even below the level of the pool.

Adam looks back at the painting he holds in his hands; he hangs it back on the wall. No matter how long he stared at it, he'd see just as much, which is nothing.

At first he might've felt tempted to believe that the painting is the kind of note that Helen never bothered to leave. But now he understands; Liv might've left the painting, but it is the building which has left him a message.

MARO

The lights don't switch on tonight. Sergei believes that it's a short circuit; he promises to resolve it by tomorrow evening. For now, there are still a few of Thea's candles left from the other night. Sergei and Anna, the first to have arrived, already lit them. They now look over Maro's shoulder, trying to see who he has smuggled in. And that's exactly how he feels; as if he trafficked Liv here, under cover of darkness.

Maro has agreed with everything that Sergei was saying about the short circuit, but only to avoid causing unnecessary stir. He knows that the lack of lights is temporary; that it has little to do with electricity. Maro reads it as the Estate's brief exertion of power; the residents deserve a lesson.

The building's known for taking care of its own; as long as the residents respect the code of conduct here. But the rules have been broken; the law of the Estate violated. For now then they have been disowned. Whatever happens in the next few days, it's on their account.

Soon after Maro arrives with Liv, the rest of the nocturnals fill the space around the pool. If they are surprised to see Liv here, they don't let on. They all greet her with the same indifferent familiarity that they usually have for each other. Only when Liv sits on the ground, everybody somehow gathers around her. Maro watches the circle that tightens around her, trying to detect the energy that surrounds Liv. It's hard to tell whether they see her as a performer who's expected to entertain them or a stranger that they study with curiosity. It's probably both, Maro thinks. It's been both for him.

Liv sits hugging her knees. A defensive, child-like pose that makes you want to wrap an arm around her back; an urge that Maro acknowledges and resists. He's hyperaware of any protective impulses he has around her; he knows her behaviour has been tailored to provoke them. Liv thrives on people's instinct to take care of her.

There are no rules, Anna says at last. Maro is impressed by how long it's taken; the silence. It was a strategic move on Liv's part; whoever speaks first reveals their motives. The other can simply respond, never disclosing their own.

Liv has waited them out. And she has won the first battle.

You just need to tell us everything, Sergei adds. Otherwise you are free to do whatever you want.

Everything? Liv asks. She's joking, but Maro can hear the undertone of worry in her voice. She's not sure where she is, who they are. And now she's told to reverse her entire pattern of behaviour; to become the one who confesses while they listen. She's used to betraying others. But in the underground she's requested to divulge her own secrets.

Is that a problem? Thea responds. Her voice is hostile; if there is someone among them perpetually resistant to stranger's charms, it's Thea. Liv, surprised, looks up to Maro.

He smiles at her reassuringly, and then turns back to Thea. He needs to warn her; Liv's one of them now, there will be no troubles. He keeps his eyes on Thea until he's certain she understood; Liv's one of them now, there will be no troubles. Only then Maro stands up from the deckchair, walks over to Liv. He breaks the circle around her; crouches in front of her.

What Anna means is that there's no need to hide anything, Maro says. He strokes her face. He shouldn't have, Maro realises the moment his hand touches her skin.

You're one of us now, he adds quickly.

And that is? Liv asks, pushing his hand away. Her tone is sharp; she's crossed her arms and does not look away. She protects herself from their interrogation with questions of her own. She doesn't really care to know; her attitude simply mirrors Thea's earlier hostility.

But what Liv happens to ask about is worth answering. It's time for them to redefine who they are, what they do here.

That's the role of a stranger; every now and then you need someone from the outside to step in and ask again about the most fundamental matters. It's not pleasant; Maro can see that Liv's question has already had an impact; the nocturnals look at each other with confusion. Who are they? They used to know; is it only now that they realise the old answers no longer hold true?

Back in the day, when they just moved around the Estate, their sleeplessness was yet another sign of their power. They were limitless; nothing could stop them. Not even their bodies, which never had to rest. During those first white nights one by one they were discovering the underground. They followed the murmur of water that had kept them awake; it lured them in.

But the inexhaustible has exhausted them; with no horizon to rest their eyes on, the undivided time has turned into a marshland. When they began to sink, there was no solid ground to hold onto; nothing to keep them on the surface. The decline might've been slow, gradual. But it has been inevitable.

The silence that now follows Liv's question proves they have begun to notice, even if they still don't understand. Maro must help them; they're his people.

He looks around. Here they are, the nocturnals. Back in the days they were all alike; indistinguishable. It is the proceeding damage that has given each of them a unique angle; left the fingerprint of tragedy. Everyone turns to ruin in their own unique own way.

To answer Liv's question, Maro then must look into each face; call them by their own names.

He starts with Thea and Titus. Their cheeks are pressed against each other. There is a superficial resemblance between them, but Maro's one of the few people who knows it's just a camouflage; these two couldn't be further apart. If anything, Titus has more in common with Adam; each feeding on their mate. Adam's sleight ascended him to the top of the Estate, but to Maro he'll always remain one of them. Helen was an artificial life support, and so was Liv.

Both Titus and Adam - they're clever enough to keep their dependencies a secret; even from themselves. They brand the dynamics as love to supress the feeling of guilt. In all fairness they remain faithful to their donors; mate for life. Titus would never look at anyone but Thea. To Adam Liv's just a projection of Helen; he even calls them by the same name. And something else about these two that Maro's nearly forgotten: their profound sense of smell.

Coyotes, Maro says out loud.

He moves onto Sergei's face who welcomes Maro's scrutiny with an unexpected smile. It exposes small, sharp teeth, throwing Maro back in time to when the three of them - Sergei, Maro and Liv - stood in front of Adam's apartment. That was the first time Maro saw Sergei smiling with his teeth; and the first time Maro noticed the eagerness and tenacity underneath Sergei's usual mask of a nihilist. It fell off temporarily when the circumstances reminded Sergei of his only real passion; breaking and entering.

Badgers, Maro says.

Next one is Anna. Every night she seems to have reached the bottom of exhaustion, until the next night comes, revealing Anna looking even more drained. Her eyes, permanently squinted, have become so small and her movements so disoriented, that from a distance Anna appears blind.

Moles, Maro says.

Now he looks back to Liv. He's ready to answer her question. But before he says anything, he pauses for the final scrutiny.

Liv's intelligent, but what really drives her is her instinct. She struggles between the thirst for freedom and a burning urge to explore her social environment.

A she-wolf, Maro thinks. There's no doubt she belongs here.

Nocturnal animals, he says aloud. That's who we are. Once we all believed we were young lions and lionesses. Nomadic and nocturnal. We didn't know that there were boundaries to our wanderings. Now all we've got is a restlessness that keeps us up at night. And that's what we do here; stay up together, helping each other to pass the time when the rest of the world unplugs, falling asleep.

Sergei unexpectedly gets on his hands and knees. In a dog-like position, he begins growling.

The sound pushes through Maro's skin; he absorbs it greedily, as if the noise feeds a starved part of him he didn't know he had.

Before Maro gets a chance to react, or even look to the others, Luca, too, gets down on the floor. He crawls around, howls. Maro sees on the faces of the others that he's not the only one who recognises the animalistic sounds; it's the battle cry of the nocturnals.

One by one, everyone joins them on the ground; barking, groaning and roaring.

The only ones standing are Maro and Liv. Hypnotised, they watch the nocturnals with a mixture of fear and fascination.

Maro turns to Liv. He says nothing, waiting for her to look at him. It takes a while, but Maro's in no rush. It's an unexpected gift, to look at her from up close at the moment when her guard is down, when she forgets herself and lets herself be seen. Every muscle of her face seems to tense up in reaction to the spectacle she watches.

But Maro knows that watching no longer suffices her; she must join in.

When Liv at last turns to Maro, he moves his face towards hers, as if in preparation for a kiss. But he stops an inch away from her lips, breathing in her breaths.

She doesn't turn away, but neither does she dare to look at him. Time passes, their breaths synchronise, the polyphonic explosion around them gains strength.

Maro doesn't know when their breaths turn into a howl, and who's the first to initiate it. But when the sound reaches their ears, they both grow silent, suddenly ashamed.

Please don't run, Maro says with his eyes. Please stay.

Liv hesitates. She breathes in, holds her breath inside. After a few seconds a prolonged cry emerges from deep inside her. Liv wails; a true she-wolf. Maro joins in. They begin laughing ecstatically; he doesn't realise when they drop on their knees.

They're a part of the cohort now; at last they belong.

LIV

Ever since she stopped sleeping, it's the first morning that Liv spends in the company of someone else.

Maro sits by her side, their arms touching. But they don't look at each other; their eyes are fixed at the window. The glass turns from opaque to transparent, as if in preparation for the morning's most spectacular show: the sunrise. It begins a few minutes later; bleeds across the sky, putting the world outside the gate on fire. The visual effects are remarkable but mean nothing here. The daily rebirth of the world outside does not apply to the Estate; the homogeneity of time here means that there are no beginnings and no ends.

A few minutes pass; can't be more than five. The sun outside recovers, plants itself into the sky, turns its bloodiness into gold. The show's over.

Liv turns away, looks at Maro. His skin shines in the morning sunlight.

He's just finished one of his workouts; the sweat covers him like a glossy suit. Liv feels an irresistible urge to press her lips against his arm; feel the taste of salt with the tip of her tongue.

She grabs an open vodka bottle from the table, gulps it. It burns her mouth, her throat.

Who are all those people? Liv asks quietly, passing Maro the bottle.

Last night? Maro asks.

Liv nods silently.

Just people, he shrugs. Like you and me.

He turns to Liv, leans forward. From up close, his features collapse, the face loses its character. She quickly scans it for any distinguishing marks. There's nothing; no moles, no scars. She looks in Maro's eyes, but he's already sealed them. Liv realises she's not the only one who understands the hazard of unexpected proximity; before moving closer, Maro secured all the potential gateways to intimacy.

Maro's drunk, his warm breath blows straight in Liv's face as he whispers: And just like us, their minds are awake. Always awake.

So they can't sleep? She wants to make sure she understood correctly.

Maro shrugs and stands up. He walks up to the punching bag, starts boxing.

Some can't, he says after a series of hooks. No matter how tired they get, their minds won't let them rest.

Liv nods; that's her. There were days when she was so exhausted she struggled holding a glass of water. Her body would enter a state of hibernation, reducing nearly all its bodily functions. And even then, her mind kept racing.

Others fall asleep, but their bodies wake up, Maro continues.

Sleepwalking? she asks.

He laughs, cross-punching the bag. Liv jumps up; she knows she's guessed correctly.

Who?! Liv exclaims.

Maro stops, looks at her. He shakes his head with scold as if to tell her that his role is to help her understand, not to betray the others' secrets. She grows quiet, large red spots suddenly take over her neck and cheeks. It surprises her. Since when has she become afraid to interrogate; ashamed to be curious? It angers her to think it's because she wants his approval. She forces herself to open her mouth again.

And you... she hears herself mumble.

But Maro's already walking away; can't hear her.

Why don't you sleep?! she shouts.

Maro pauses; turns back. He stares at Liv with bewilderment.

You really want to know?

Liv nods. He walks back towards her. She doesn't know why she feels as if he wanted to hit her. But instead of covering herself, she clenches her hands in fists. It's the second thing this morning she learns about herself. She might want to crave his approval, but if he wanted to hurt her, she would fight back.

But the strike never arrives. Instead, Maro leans forward.

There are certain things you cannot unlearn, remember? he whispers in her ear. He straightens up. If you excuse me, he says, about to leave.

But their eyes meet again. It's an accident.

My body and mind need to be kept awake, at all times, Maro blurts. He looks around anxiously, both surprised to have said it and afraid that someone might hear him.

But why? she asks. Too soon.

I don't deserve to rest, he says and this time disappears from the room before she manages to ask him yet another question.

He's done well, Liv thinks. Very well. He didn't lie, and yet he's told me nothing.

ADAM

The cover of the book is matte and lacks colour; he can't see why anyone would pick it from the shelf. Maybe the title; it's not bad. 'A Possible Husband' holds a promise of letting the reader into a ruthless scrutiny, in which intimate details and human flaws will be exposed, mocked. He can see that's something most people would enjoy.

But the book is good. Adam feels a sense of relief, pride even. After all, he's the one who picked Liv, asked her to move in. And she's turned out to be a fine stranger.

There's something else. She didn't leave him; not quite. She's just finished a project. And even then, she's still left something behind.

He hears a faint creak; someone walks in. The creak is a post-Liv addition; before her all doors in the Estate closed and opened without a sound. He's not sure why the building let her do it; introduce change. But just like with the painting, Adam's inclined to believe it's part of a more personal message. No longer can he count on the building to remain safe. He must act alone; rely on his own strength.

Adam takes his eyes away from the book and turns around vigilantly.

Liv...? he says.

There is no response; just the sound of approaching footsteps. He runs through the rehearsed speech. She must say yes; she owes him that.

The footsteps get louder; in a second she'll be here. Adam's heart speeds up; he presses the book closer to his chest.

Then something shifts. The smell that hits his nostrils is familiar but does not belong to Liv. It's a synthetic perfume, not a natural bodily odour. He imagines that now she's left she might wear a cologne that he does not know. But she would never choose a perfume which literally punches you in the face with dark, woody notes; it's too accurate, too revealing. A perfume is a dream of oneself, not a portrait. And Liv dreams of being unseen, camouflaged.

Alice walks in. He was right to recognise the aroma; it's the same fragrance she wore when she came over for dinner.

Adam sighs, exhaling a mixture of disappointment and relief. Straight away he regrets the instinct; he now can't escape supplementing the lacking oxygen, breathing in Alice's perfume.

The door was open, Alice says.

I left it open, Adam says. In case she came back.

Alice does not respond, but sits on the floor opposite Adam. It doesn't suit her; Alice is not someone who can comfortably sit on the floor; she's too self-conscious. She keeps her legs and back straight, using her hands to support herself. Her body forms an 'L'; a human chair.

You didn't come to work, Alice says.

I was a little busy... Adam says, pointing at the book.

Alice leans forward and gently takes the book of Adam's hands; he lets her. She flips through it. Adam watches her face. She was stressed when she walked in; now she's worried. He sees her anxiety as clearly as her efforts to conceal it.

You really got into it, didn't you... Alice observes. She points to the open pages.

Adam shrugs. Sure, he's underlined a bit of text or circled some words. There might be a couple of notes he wrote on the margins, when the writing prompted him to add a comment or an exclamation mark. But it's a good book; it deserves a focused reading.

He takes the book out of Alice's hands. If she doesn't understand, she doesn't deserve to hold it.

Have you read it? he asks, convinced she'll say no.

I have, Alice says.

It's pretty good, no? Adam asks.

It's well written, yes, she says.

Adam pauses. He's tempted to tell her, even though he's certain she won't understand. But he's been rehearsing in his mind for so long, it feels reasonable to test saying it out loud.

Do you think that now... Adam begins, quietly. That she might, you know... write something like this about me?

I wouldn't worry, Alice says.

Why not? Adam snaps. Do you think I'm not interesting enough to inspire a novel?

That's not what I meant, Adam...she says. She reaches out to squeeze Adam's hand but he's faster; how dare she try to touch him again.

It's just that after what happened, Alice begins. She points to the book. To that guy, you know. I doubt she'll be very keen to mix life and fiction...again...

She wasn't at first, sure, Adam agrees. But it's been quite some time since she arrived here... she might come to miss it.

Didn't you say she broke every pen in your house? Alice reminds him. Doesn't really look like someone who craves writing... And that computer she crushed?

Exactly! Adam exclaims. She wouldn't have done that if she wasn't afraid to start writing again. 'If your hand causes you to stumble, cut it off and throw it away'.

Adam. You're quoting the Bible, Alice says.

Thank you for stopping by, he says and gets up. But it wasn't necessary.

Alice snorts. Adam realises that for the first time he truly hates her. In a certain way she's succeeded; she managed to make him feel something.

He walks up to the corridor and opens the door. It's the only way to get her out.

Alice shakes her head with disbelief but stands up.

I'll be back at work tomorrow, Adam says when she approaches the door. She halts to look in his face. She finds something that surprises her; she watches him for a while as if to confirm she's right.

Wait... Alice says, watching him carefully. Do you want her to write about you?

Not about me, he says. He takes a deep breath, readying himself to say it.

I want her to write about Helen.

MARO

The electricity in the underground hasn't come back yet. Sergei apologises for failing to resolve the problem. But Maro knows that he couldn't have even begun fixing it; there's never been anything objectively wrong. Sergei's disappointment makes Maro wonder how different each of their relationships must be with the Estate. It crosses his mind that everything he knows about this place might as well be a story he just tells himself.

But whatever the reason behind the electricity cut, if they want to stay here tonight for hours to come, they must get new candles. There is something unnerving about being here together without the lights; Maro feels as if they cannot fully trust each other. The electric lights they're used to switching on at night are not just to let them see; they're to disperse the darkness that creeps inside each of them.

When Thea and Titus arrive with a new supply of candles, everybody rushes to help them. The flames illuminate the space, the air seems denser. The contours of the faces smudge, the features morph depending on the angle from which they're lit.

The change in the underground's lighting also affects the setting. Before they would all spread across the space, each minding their own business. Their interactions were casual, took place whenever their paths crossed.

Now they all rest by the pool. Side by side, they face the

water. But Maro knows that if the electricity cut lasts few days longer, they will begin sitting in a circle, looking not in space, but at each other. Without other distractions, all they'll have left will be each other's company. And there's already a new intensity to their dynamic; they're hyperaware of each other's presence. As if expectant of a still enigmatic, but imminently approaching, explosion.

Maro realises it's not just the light. The physical change to their setting has only emphasised the difference between the way they were before Liv entered the underground, and how they are now. But it's not her presence that triggered the change; that alone has brought a refreshment but couldn't have shaken their foundation. It's the question she's asked; the answer she's been given. It made them believe they're more than a group of insomniacs who gather by the pool. They see themselves as a distinct species now; the nocturnal animals.

LIV

Natasha is the first to look away from the pool. She lifts herself up on her forearms, turns to Maro. Liv watches her from the corner of her eye, sees how Natasha's eyes linger on Maro's face. As if she was waiting for him to ask her to come over. To lie down by him, the way they probably used to before Liv has arrived. She imagines it must be unusual for Natasha who doesn't look like someone accustomed to asking for permission; people like her do what they want. But she must've heard that Liv has moved into Maro's apartment; she probably wonders now which of the old arrangements still hold.

And so does he, it seems, as Maro quickly gets up and walks away. He glances at Liv to check whether she's noticed anything. But she's turned away, pretends to be eavesdropping on Anna's and Thea's drowsy conversation.

It's not even a conversation; more a fusion of isolated monologues, which each woman recites without opening their eyes. It has a certain resemblance to a verbal exchange as the women lie side by side and never speak at the same time.

I want to play a game! Natasha's cry unexpectedly explodes in the room. Liv sees that Maro halts; he turns back to Natasha.

Here we go again, Anna mumbles without opening her eyes.

But I want to play the dream game, Natasha demands.

Haven't we had enough of that already? Anna says.

Never, Natasha responds. I love this game. Just as much as you hate it.

Liv now looks to Maro for explanation. 'A game?' she tries to ask him without words. But Maro just shrugs his shoulders. As if he didn't know what they're talking about.

Liv notices that Natasha's move surprised him. Her tone is innocent, she hasn't looked once in his direction. But whatever the game is, she wants to play it to annoy Maro, Liv's certain of that. And maybe to hurt her.

But no one else seems to sense the undercurrent of their dynamics. Instead, they exchange suggestive looks, pointing to Liv. She ignores the attention, waiting for Maro to give some clues. She's capable of making her own decisions, she just wants some background information; some advice. But Maro stands as if paralysed, unable to make up his own mind.

Liv's never played... Luca says.

Liv tries to think of a way out, but before she gets to open her mouth, Thea exclaims:

Oh, you'll love it, you'll love it so much!

How very exciting... Alex says to himself. But then he turns to Maro, rolling his eyes. And even though Maro doesn't say a word, Liv feels as if they were talking about her behind her back.

So how does it work? Liv asks.

You just have to tell us your dreams, Anna says.

She doesn't exactly 'have to'... Maro says, at last coming to her defence. But Liv glares at him; it's too late now.

Oh, but you must tell us! Natasha insists.

I wouldn't mind, Liv says. It's just that I don't dream. Or sleep. Isn't that the point of everyone here?

Oh, no, not from now! Thea laughs. The dreams from before!

You can choose a category, Sergei says. Favourite dreams. Recurring dreams. Most disturbing dreams.

The last dream, Maro says.

Liv turns to Maro, surprised. Is that what you want to know? she wonders. And if so, couldn't you just ask?

All right, she agrees. The last dream then.

Everybody gets up, moves closer. They gather in front of Liv as if in a cinema, before a much anticipated screening. Suddenly her palms sweat, heart races. It's stage fright, she realises. She doesn't know why but the realisation amuses her, taking away the stress. She clears her throat.

I don't remember when it was exactly... she begins.

That's fine, absolutely fine, Thea reassures her. Just go on.

Was it here? Alex asks.

No. It must've been the last night before. The night of the party. Liv says. I never managed to sleep properly again after that, just an hour here or there, out of pure exhaustion. But no dreams, no.

Everybody nods silently. Natasha smiles her sweetest smile, encouraging Liv to continue. Strangely, it works.

It's just so silly, she laughs. Now that I think about it... it doesn't make any sense, really.

It's a dream, Maro says. They always do and do not make sense at the same time.

He gently runs his hand across Liv's arm.

Go on, Maro says.

I really doubt that it's all that interesting... Liv hesitates. She sees the impatience on their faces. But fine, here it is. The dream.

Liv pauses and looks around. Everybody's eyes are fixed on her. She suddenly realises how excited she feels. It's a well-known thrill, one she hasn't experienced since she's moved here. And one she thought she wouldn't experience ever again. But here she is, telling her story in front of an audience.

There were three women, all of different ages, somewhere between twenty and fifty. And I was all three of them at the same time. They... we... We were on a journey.

I love it, I love it already! Thea whispers, mesmerised. She turns to Titus. Don't you just love it? she asks.

Titus nods and smiles encouragingly at Liv.

Right... Liv says, slightly disoriented. She's not used to interacting with readers; not when she's in the middle of telling the story. Where were we? she asks.

On a journey! Sergei reminds her.

On a journey, yes... Liv now remembers. Our task was to move quickly from the place where we were to the next one. But as we rushed along the road, we took a wrong turn and found ourselves in a forest. It was a large, old forest with very tall trees. We stopped and looked around, having no idea where to go next. Then suddenly a large, brown hare stood in front of us.

A rabbit! Anna exclaims. Of course, there was a rabbit...

A hare, not a rabbit, Sergei corrects her.

Shh! I can't wait to hear it! Natasha silences them.

The hare... Liv continues. He offered to show us the way out. I... I mean we, or one of the 'I's' that I felt I was at that point, didn't want to listen. I kept saying to myself 'You're a hare, you cannot talk, you cannot hear this'.

But he did, right? Luca asks with hope.

Yes, he did, Liv confirms. And he grew really angry and said 'Oh, really? Well then, look to the left!'. And we all looked, and from the left there was a horde of beastly, angry bears coming our way. So without thinking, we followed the hare. And we jumped into this long, dusty tunnel, and ended up in a closed, stuffy room somewhere underground. I looked around and realised only two of us were left. One of the women had gone missing. Crying out in anger I attacked the hare, charging him with lies. Instead of showing us the way to the airport, we were trapped with no hope of escape.

Un-fucking-believable! Sergei exclaims. What a sneaky bastard!

Is that it? Maro asks. Your dream ended with you being trapped?

Not quite, Liv admits, looking straight into Maro's eyes. She will not look away until the end of her tale.

The hare smiled ironically and muttered 'Look to the left', Liv continues. And there was a large glass window, and behind it was a large airport, with planes taking off every second. I felt hope rising in me again. The last thing I remember were the mocking words of the hare 'And now you've just got to find a way out of here...'

THE STORY

LIV

She lies down in the living room, her body sinks into the floor. She likes not having a bed here. Having a bed would be like keeping your running shoes after you lost any ability to move your legs. Putting them on would resemble placing an insomniac body in bed, a painful reminder of what's been taken away.

Liv appreciates how empty Maro's apartment is. There are no mock-ups here, no souvenirs. She prefers the discomfort of the floor, it's accurate. That's how a rest feels when you cannot sleep; sore, incomplete.

From behind the wall she hears the sounds of Maro stepping out of the bath, walking through the corridor, entering the bedroom. Her hearing has rapidly sharpened over the last few days. It might be linked to the ongoing electricity cuts during the nights. She once read a study that mice kept in the darkness become unusually sensitive to sounds. The brain adapts to the lack of light by strengthening the connections between neurons. The improvement in hearing compensates for the impaired vision.

Liv liked that study, just as she likes all stories of deprivation causing the body to step up. She believes that is how all talents are born, as a form of reimbursement. There are no refunds, but life is kind enough to sometimes offer an exchange on the damaged functions.

Like a mouse kept in the darkness, Liv now hears every sound of Maro getting dressed. The fabric of his trousers rubbing against his skin, the zipper moving upward, to close the fly, the belt which hits a metal button.

He's almost ready. In a minute or two he will leave the apartment and step into the underground. Liv will not follow him, not tonight. They haven't spoken since last night, since she told them the dream. Just as she delivered the final lines, she realised she was tricked. The shared dream weakened her position among the nocturnals, made her look like someone who's on their way out from here. Liv knows that everyone's status in the Estate is tentative. Hers suddenly appeared as temporary, without an option to stay.

Maro must've sensed that too; he made it easy for her to avoid any interaction. He simply continued his usual routine, allowing Liv to anticipate his moves. Giving her the space to avoid him. The day has passed without them crossing paths.

But the night is harder. Liv feels an urge to step in the underground; a longing. She'd swear she keeps hearing a splash of water, the same one she's heard every night since she stopped sleeping; the one that lured her into the underground. She'd told Maro about it; he knew exactly what she was talking about. She wasn't alone; all the nocturnals have claimed to hear the water before they discovered the underground pool. But whatever they heard couldn't have reached them from the outside; it must've resonated inside of them.

She hears Maro opening the door, walking out. She hoped he would halt by the door. And if not call out to her, then at least hesitate about whether he should. But all his movements are determined, precise; there is no space left for doubt. As the door closes after Maro, Liv realises she's never been left alone at night in the Estate. First there was Adam sleeping behind the wall, then there were the nocturnals. And Maro.

Now it's just her and the building. Liv closes her eyes; tunes in. After a while her breath becomes very steady, rhythmical. The breath of a person sleeping.

Liv sits up, pressing her hand against her mouth. It's not possible, she couldn't have... She didn't.

The breath she's just heard continues its rhythmical pace; and it's not her own. She stands up, walks towards the wall. She presses her ear against it; the sound of the breathing intensifies. Just to be sure she places her flat palms on the surface. The wall fluctuates beneath her touch, downward and up, matching precisely the rhythm of the sound.

Liv has no doubt; the sound belongs to the building. And now she understands; the residents do not sleep so that the Estate can rest.

MARO

Never before has he been here alone at night. But the persistent lack of light and Liv's unexpected absence had the group disperse halfway through the night. No one dared ask Maro what happened; not even Natasha. But he would catch them glimpsing at the entrance longingly, with hope. He once caught himself stealing a glance in the same direction.

But Liv didn't show up. The darkness persisted and when the candles, one by one, began going out, the nocturnals, too, retreated. Maro knew that they had nowhere else to go, and if tomorrow night the situation repeats itself, they will stay. But tonight the disappointment was too strong; they'd rather wander around the Estate, directionless, than stay here.

Maro would have probably followed in their steps if it wasn't for Alex's guitar. Walking back and forth across the room to pass the time, he nearly tripped over the abandoned instrument. He crouched to check the damage and that was it. The moment he took the guitar in his hands, it all came back. The music, no longer pouring through his headphones now burst from inside of him. Maybe it wasn't even him playing; maybe the guitar was playing itself.

He doesn't know how much time passed, and what time it can be now. Not even whether it's still night or the day has already begun. All he knows is that Liv stands in front of him. The flashlight from her phone gives her the appearance of a night-time vision; an apparition.

Their eyes meet; Liv comes a few steps closer.

Maro looks up and smiles at Liv, continuing to play the guitar.

Where is everybody? Liv whispers.

Maro doesn't answer; not with words. But he changes the melody; begins playing a song, in which he finally tells her things. He can't tell whether she hears him, and if so, whether she likes what she hears. But she doesn't leave; for now it's all that matters.

When he finishes playing, he puts down the guitar and walks up to Liv. He halts right in front of her.

Maro looks into her face, waiting for her to let him see her. Liv turns her head away.

But she doesn't move and so Maro gently grabs her chin. He moves her head back in his direction. She leans forward to kiss him. But instead of her lips, he reaches for her hands, hidden in the sleeves of her jumper.

Liv instantly pulls them away, but Maro forces them back. He unwraps the hands from the sleeves, opens her fists. He takes her hands in his hands. She releases the pressure. Her hands look like old wounds; there are hardly any nails left, the cuticles are bleeding. The skin is scratched and stained. Maro cannot believe he's never noticed Liv's hands before; it couldn't have just happened over a couple of days.

He lifts a hand to his lips and kisses it. He puts her fingers into his mouth, one after another. When he finishes with one hand, he takes the other, and repeats it.

When Maro finishes caressing Liv's hands, he takes off her sweater and her bra. She again makes a step forward, but he holds her at arm's length. Maro knows that Liv doesn't mind letting him or anyone else in; what she doesn't want is someone standing beside her, watching. That's the role she's ascribed to herself; changing places makes her feel vulnerable. Feeling vulnerable makes her run. But Maro would rather have her run than compromise.

He doesn't want her close until she lets him see her.

And she understands. The hands, at first crossed across her chest, fall down. Liv looks at him; smiles. She takes a deep breath and closes her eyes.

Maro walks a bit closer and puts his hand between her thighs. Maro does not embrace Liv. He looks her in the eyes and unzips her trousers. He puts his hand inside. His face is very close, but he continues to keep Liv at arm's length. He avoids her lips. After a while Liv grabs Maro's face in two hands and pulls it close to her; this time she won't let him pull back. And so he lets her kiss him.

LIV

He's covered Liv with her sweater. It's not even hers; it's his. She took it from his closet, put it on, made it hers. That's what she does; walks into men's lives with nothing of her own. Then she makes their homes, their belongings, hers. But just for a little while; there's always an expiry date. When she leaves, she takes nothing with her. Nothing but the story. But this one she extracts, patiently sculpting it in her hands. Such a story becomes her story; her baby. And it's that one thing she could never leave behind.

Tell me something about you, Liv says.

Maro begins laughing. He lights up a cigarette, inhales.

Just because we can't sleep, doesn't mean we have to talk, he says.

She takes the cigarette out of his mouth and turns away. Maro strokes her hair.

What would you like to know? he asks gently.

Liv shrugs her shoulders.

Something... she says.

She puts down the cigarette, even if it's not finished. She turns back to Maro. She runs one of her fingertips across his face.

Anything...she begins. That no one else knows.

You always want to know that! he snorts. Sooner or later, you all do. But already, now?

Liv moves away. She feels furious with him; fury lets her

139

avoid feeling pain. She's surprised how much Maro's words hurt her. It's not that there have been other women, but that there were other women like her. She rolls up, about to walk away. But Maro grabs Liv; moves on top of her. He lifts himself on his forearms and studies her face carefully.

Something that no one knows, huh? Maro says.

Liv keeps silent, suddenly scared. He looks very tense; he's searching for something in her face. Whatever it is, he doesn't find it. Resigned, he moves to the side.

He lights another cigarette and for a while smokes in silence.

Be careful what you wish for, he says and closes his eyes.

MARO

He wonders how long he'll have to keep his eyes shut for the images to come back. But it's almost immediate; as if they were right behind the door he had locked years ago, just waiting to be let in.

The large bedroom is lit with moonlight. It's a beautiful bedroom in a beautiful house; the most beautiful house in the neighbourhood of beautiful houses. It's a place that does not know of the Estate, and if it knew, it wouldn't have believed in it. Across a wide, wooden bed sleeps Emily; his wife.

Maro does not lie by her side. He stands in the doorway, naked. He removed his clothes in the kitchen, but he does not remember it.

His eyes are wide open as he stares blankly ahead of him. He sees, must see something, and yet he's blind. He's asleep; he's awake.

He walks towards the bed; his movements somewhat robotic. He halts by the window, standing in the moonlight for a long while, as if frozen. There is no objective reason why he would stand there. In hindsight he likes to think that the moon was an alarm for his intuition. It shouted at him, tried to wake him up. But there was no evidence of what happened during the several minutes he stood naked in the moonlight. No one could've known what he felt; especially not him.

Maybe if he stayed there longer, if the moon had more time, nothing would've happened that night. The cry from the inside would be loud enough to wake him up. But Emily wakes up first.

She opens her eyes; stares at her husband's silhouette. She smiles and lifts herself on her forearms.

Have you been having trouble sleeping? Emily asks. Must be the full moon.

At first, Maro does not move, then slowly he turns around.

Come to bed, won't you? Emily smiles.

She lifts up the sheets in a welcoming gesture, disclosing her naked body. Exactly at the same moment Maro stretches out his hands and wraps them around Emily's neck. She tries to fight him but fails. He's always had strong hands; it's these hands that made him an exceptional musician. Emily never stood a chance.

There is a slight crack, as if he broke a thin chicken bone. He doesn't know how long he holds her, but longer than necessary. He's exhausted; at last passing out next to his wife.

Maro opens his eyes. That's right, that's the internal footage he shot seven years ago while listening to the lawyers fighting in court. They informed him that he could not remember a thing from that night; he was deeply asleep. But they lied. During the trial he accepted the account they presented as his memory. He experienced the events second by second, archived them. He hasn't forgotten the tiniest detail since.

The cigarette in his hand has turned into ash, without Maro taking a single drag. He puts it down; turns around to face Liv.

I woke up like this, he says. With her dead body in my arms.

But... You were free? she begins.

I was never found guilty, Maro says. It was decided I was not awake, he says. Not in control of my actions. In the eyes of the law I bore no responsibility.

Maro reaches out for another cigarette. He lights it, for a while playing with the smoke.

No responsibility, no guilt, he continues. And so I was discharged.

And that was it?! Liv asks. How could you...

Go on living? he finishes her sentence.

Liv grows silent and stares at Maro with terror.

You're right, he agrees. How could I? Well, at first I entertained the option of joining her. That would have been a great way out, wouldn't it? But more like a reward, really. And I didn't deserve one. What was I to do then? But she, she knew. One night I woke up, hearing her whisper.

Maro leans forward. He turns Liv's head to the side, runs his lips from her bare shoulder to her ear.

'Sleep no more!' he whispers.

Liv shivers and pulls away. She stares at Maro with not just dread, but revulsion. As if he was a monster. She's right; he is a monster.

How is that for a story? he laughs bitterly. He leans forward, strokes her hair.

Liv jumps up; steps back.

Oh, I see, he says. Now you're appalled. You can't let me touch you. Not a man who murdered his own wife.

A tear runs down Liv's face. She says nothing, turns around and starts moving towards the exit. Maro jumps up and runs after her. He blocks the door.

So that's it? he asks. Now that you got your story, you know something that no one else does - certainly no one here - you're just going to leave?

It's never 'just' when it comes to leaving, Liv says quietly. You know that.

But you are leaving, he repeats.

I have to, she says.

You don't 'have to', Maro says.

I must go, she says quietly. Maro has no doubt she means it. He steps away, freeing the exit.

Well, if you really must, he says. Anyway, you've never really been more than a daydream, have you?

LIV

At first she runs up the stairs, but with every stride her pace slows down. She wishes it was the stairs' fault; that their steps would grow higher, become impossible to climb. Or unexpectedly slippery, as if made of ice. But the Estate's omnipresence seems to have left them. They're all alone here now. No one's watching.

It's all her legs then; they're heavy, nearly immobile. She struggles to lift them, to push forward. She needs all her strength to keep moving; it feels as if her body switched to slow motion. Maybe her body is done with obeying the mind, executing its crimes. Maybe this time it chooses to side with her heart. Two against one. Still, it's a lost battle for them. Liv's no less skilled than Maro; she knows how to tame her body, her heart. And so she climbs one more step, then another one. Just keep walking, she whispers, keep walking away.

But once she reaches the hall, she freezes. The exit is right in front of her. Ten, maybe fifteen steps. Even if she had to crawl, she would've reached the door in a couple of minutes. And then another couple of minutes to reach the gate. In less than five minutes she would've left the Estate behind; would've walked back to where she came from. The outside world is at her fingertips; no one's stopping her. And yet Liv stands still.

It's not that she doesn't want to go; leaving is all that she wants. She just can't make her legs move. It's not a paralysis though; it's a dissent. She's heard it can happen sometimes; willpower is like a muscle. Every now and then, you need to give it a rest. Pull back on the demands, let the body roam freely for a while.

Liv's sure she's read it somewhere; and that she's never thought it could've applied to her. As if she didn't even consider a will to be an autonomous organ. She was her will, her will was her. Heartless and bodiless, but wilful. The nature of her mind has always been that of an auteur; it orchestrated every element of her life. But now it's left with nothing but a vision; the actors rebelled and won't perform.

Fine, she thinks. If going back is what you want, so be it. I won't stop you. Go.

The legs start moving. It's a steady, firm pace. But to Liv's astonishment, they're not walking down. They're climbing up the stairs once again. Faster and faster, until they run.

They halt with the same resolve that had them fly the stairs before. Liv looks; she's in front of Adam's apartment. The door is ajar.

It's early morning, but not early enough for Adam to still be home. She walks up to the door, pushes it slightly. The door opens.

Liv and her body are no longer disjointed. Walking in doesn't happen against her will; it's something she, too, wants.

She walks around the apartment to check whether Adam is in. Or anyone else. Alice, or maybe even someone new. A stranger, just like she was.

But the place is empty. Emptier than it's ever been. Something that used to be here, that kept her company when Adam was asleep, when he was at work, is no longer here.

The only cameras left are Liv's eyes, scanning the once familiar space. The bed, the sofa, the bare walls. Her painting is gone; Adam must've taken it off the wall. She walks up to where she hung the picture. The tiny hole left by the nail is still there; the wall refused to heal. She touches it with her finger. Now she knows why she's here; why she had to return. To touch the tiny scar is her victory; to see that she has left a mark.

But the apartment hides another reminder of Liv's power to change the world around her. Not just change; destroy it.

The box with the pen cartridges is exactly where she hid it; the kitchen drawer, together with cleavers and the sharpest knives. An apt place for the bullets, and an unlikely one to be looked into. No one in this house has ever cooked; none of its elaborate equipment has ever been used. Except the knife that served Liv as a nail to hang her picture.

Liv's hands shake when she opens the drawer, takes out the cartridges.

Carrying the cartridges on an open hand she walks out of the kitchen. There is nothing else holding her here, she must now leave the Estate.

But as she passes the living room she notices a pile of paper. Blank paper. The pile is thick, at least a couple of hundred. Hundreds of empty pages. She knows straight away it's a trap. But she doesn't know what happens next.

She finds herself on the ground, her cheek is pressed against the floor, her head heavy, exploding with dull, nauseating pain. There is a strange sound, as if rhythmical. Liv opens her eyes with effort. A pair of male shoes walks around her nervously. She tries to move onto her back to look up. She first sees the dark fabric of suit trousers, then a familiar overcoat. She doesn't have to look up to know. She shuts her eyes rapidly; there's hope that a moment of blankness can erase what Liv hopes to be the phantom of her mind.

But when she opens her eyes, Adam crouches in front of her. He smiles; it's a smile that Liv's never seen. Adam's beaming.

I knew you'd be back, he says.

ADAM

Never before has Adam watched Liv asleep. She doesn't look peaceful; more like a child with a high fever that fights for every breath. She's probably not even asleep but in a state of delirium. She sweats heavily, whispers unintelligible words and sentences. But Adam doesn't feel alarmed; there is not a hint of sickness in her smell. Her defence system is dormant; there are no bacteria or viruses to be fought. And yet Adam has noticed a slight change in Liv's odour; it's more aggressive. Arousing even. Maybe writing triggers in her body a similar reaction to sex.

But the fever itself is caused by pure exhaustion. The entire floor is covered in hand-written pieces of paper. Anyone would begin hallucinating after working at such a pace. It might even be the place where all writers end after finishing a story; delirious and flat on the floor. He wouldn't have known; it's the first time he's witnessed a creative process.

He was right though. To make her stay not through force, but her own free will was a brilliant idea. It's almost surprising to see Liv take the bait so blindly, to follow through on the task so completely. But then again, it must've been something she'd been craving since the day she stepped into his apartment. He just made the drug available, placed it right in front of her.

Liv jerks rapidly and turns on her back. Adam halts. Until now he hadn't even realised he'd been pacing around the room, waiting for her to wake up.

She opens her eyes and tries to look up, but shuts them

146

before she gets to see Adam. He crouches by her side. She might be weak, in need of help.

Liv opens her eyes again and looks at Adam. There isn't a trace of surprise in her face. As if she's already known it's him. As if she needn't look, but could have sensed his presence.

Adam experiences a moment of thrill that he's never felt around her before; it's a sudden belief in their absolute connection at this moment. They might not belong together, but they have come to truly know each other. Now Adam's almost certain she will not refuse him. And in return, he will let her go.

How long have I been here? Liv asks.

Not sure when you arrived... he says. I got home a couple of hours ago and found you here, sleeping on the floor.

Liv tries to get up, but straight away her face cringes with pain. She grabs her head with both hands. Adam too, winces, imagining how she must feel. He's always had a very low tolerance to physical suffering, and there's nothing more excruciating than a headache. Poor Liv. He stretches out his hand to stroke her head, but Liv pulls away abruptly before he manages to touch her.

You must've drugged me... she says. I don't sleep, remember?

You do now, he says. Adam smiles to stress he's delivering good news. But Liv responds with hostility; suspicion even. As if she had no memory of what happened here; of what she had done.

But the proof is all around them. Adam spreads his arms to help Liv notice her surroundings. She takes a look at last; they're like two tiny boats in the sea of paper. Adam picks up a couple of pages.

It actually makes a lot of sense, he says, pointing to her writing. Just think about it, Liv. You stopped sleeping exactly when you stopped writing. Everything that you would normally pour into your work had to be stored in your head. No wonder you couldn't sleep.

LIV

She leans forward pausing just a couple of inches away from the page. She studies the writing for a long time. As if she was presented with a counterfeit; a fake note. Slowly, the suspicion turns into disbelief. She touches the paper, lets her fingertips follow the shape of letters and words. The movement triggers something inside her; an uprising of recollections. The events happened only a few hours ago, but then they disappeared in a marshland of memory. As if she had a blackout, a short memory failure.

Liv's hands imitate the movement of writing; the memories crawl back to the surface. They are deformed, covered in mud. Still, she begins to recognise them.

Liv takes the pages in her hands. Her ink stained fingertips leave an imprint on the paper; a watermark of authenticity. She's certain; the pages are her own.

I really wrote that... she says.

Yes, you did, Adam says. You really wrote that! And now I want you to write something else. For me.

Liv shudders at the sound of Adam's voice; she's almost forgotten he was here. But his request comes as no surprise. That's what people used to want from her; to write for or about them. And the only stories she wanted to tell were of people who demanded privacy.

She tries to fight off the smile before she turns to Adam. It's not that she thinks there isn't a part of his life worth recording. It's that she never expected someone like him to take any interest in storytelling. To see its value, urgency.

What is it that you'd like me to write? she asks, her eyes glued to the pages. She's not yet ready to look at him, aware she might give into temptation and laugh in his face.

Helen's story, he says.

She now turns to Adam with earnestness. His face is burning. It's not just excitement; it's madness.

Run! the voice inside her screams. Run now, before he gets to say anything else, before it might be too late.

Liv jumps up. But once again, she fails to leave. It's not her legs; they can't wait to start moving. It takes Liv all her newly regained willpower to make them stand still. Just as her legs refused to execute her orders, she now refuses to follow their instinct.

Instead of heading straight for the door, she walks around the room, picking up the pieces of paper and putting them together. She hands the manuscript to Adam.

Here you go, she says. Helen's story.

But that's not... Adam begins.

I'm Helen. And this is my story, Liv interrupts him. Isn't that what you asked for? Helen's story?

Adam drops the manuscript. Before the pages once again land on the floor, they fly around the room like seagulls. Liv's sure she can hear their cry; the squawking and the wailing.

I meant a real one, Adam says.

Real Helen or real story? Liv asks. She takes her eyes off the disregarded pages; forces herself to look at Adam.

Listen, it's the only thing I want... he begins. Before...before... Adam tries to continue but falters. His lips are now so pale that Liv struggles to imagine they're capable of finishing the sentence. Or uttering any other words.

He closes his eyes. It looks as if he is shutting a door and venturing to the storeroom to search for the missing words.

After a while Adam's eyes open; he's back.

Before you leave me, he says. Together with words he seems to have found composure; some kind of peace even. His voice is gentle but firm; the sentence ends with a clear full stop. There is no hope that Liv will deny it, prove him wrong. Adam knows who she is and that she will leave.

But he demands compensation. Liv sees the irony of his unexpected demand. For years it used to be her who wanted to leave with a story. And now again she is being asked to leave a story behind. It was different with Robert, sure. He wanted Liv to abandon her story, to choose him over her book. Adam's request is more modest; reasonable even. He lets Liv go, lets her take her story. All that he's asking is that he, too, gets something in return.

Robert. His name prompts a series of images. Flashbacks. Liv shudders. It can't be.

She quickly lifts up her ink stained hands; examines the skin.

I broke it... Liv mutters.

Huh? Adam asks.

I broke the cartridge... Liv says.

But Adam doesn't hear her. And even if he did, how could he understand?

She was a lot like you... he begins.

Liv slumps on the floor.

She also couldn't sleep... From the very first night that she moved here with me, Adam continues.

Liv can't take her eyes off her stained skin. She rubs her hands against each other. Not to remove the ink, but to feel it.

She kept begging me to find a new house but I ... Adam says.

Without looking at him, Liv understands he's telling her his story. Helen's story. The story he wants Liv to write.

I wouldn't listen. I couldn't afford to listen to her. Day by day she was turning into a ghost, but I... I pretended not to notice. Then suddenly everything changed. She still wouldn't sleep, but it no longer bothered her. Instead, she looked invigorated. I knew she had found the others.

Liv suddenly jerks and turns her gaze from her fingertips

to Adam's face.

The others? Liv asks. Could he have known all along?

Don't look so surprised, he says. I used to be one of you.
Until I met Helen.

Adam sits down on the floor across from Liv. They're
surrounded by the dozens of pages Liv used to tell Helen's
story. And now she's going to hear what really happened.

There's this legend within our community... Adam says.
He lowers his voice, drawing Liv closer.

Those who can't sleep can't love, Adam whispers. Their
hearts are broken, their minds weary.

Adam pauses; shrugs.

I never thought much of it. But then on the first night I
brought her here I slept like a baby.

She didn't... Liv says.

No, he says. But once she found out she wasn't alone, I
thought it was a fair trade. She helped me pass my nights,
they helped her with hers. And the days, the days were ours.
I never worked so little in my life! I would be the last to enter
the office and the first to leave.

But it wasn't enough... Liv says.

Maybe, Adam says. Or maybe something happened.
Something down there, by the pool.

Maro; the first thought that comes to Liv's mind. Not that
he would hurt Helen. Not after what happened to his wife.
He's paid too high a price; he's still paying. But why would
he never tell Liv that he knew Helen? That she was one of
them? Just like... Me, Liv thinks. Helen was just like me. I
wasn't just a sub for Adam. I was a sub for Maro.

One night I woke up to find her right there, Adam points
to the bedroom. In our bed, deeply asleep. I couldn't be
happier. But she, she was in despair. Sleeping meant she
could no longer be a part of the underground. And that
would've been the end of Helen. But she wasn't someone
who gave up easily. And she found a way. She slept all day

long. At first I didn't make much of it. She had the right, didn't she? After months of staying awake. My sleeping beauty, that's what I called her. She was asleep when I got back from work, asleep when I woke up. I didn't have the heart to wake her. I thought that once her body got enough of it, regenerated, we'd be able to enjoy each other again.

I knew that for a while she still continued going to the underground. She would fall asleep by my side; set an alarm to wake up just a couple of hours later. I didn't like what she was doing; swapping our days for their nights. I didn't say a word though. I let her choose. I didn't like her choice, sure. I hoped it would change. But I respected it was hers to make.

Liv watches Adam with disbelief; there's little resemblance between the man she's lived with all these weeks and the one that now sits across from her, telling this story. A part of her regrets not knowing him. But Liv knows better than to trust the melancholy that stories trigger. She gives Adam the credit for his narrative skills; that's the only credit she knows he deserves.

They weren't so generous, it turned out. Not sure how they found out, but once they did, Helen was banned from the underground. I admit I was happy to have her by my side. Until that morning when I woke up and she was gone. Just like that, Adam snaps his fingers.

The flick is like the hand movement at the end of hypnosis; Liv snaps out of her trance. And just like at the end of hypnosis, Liv feels slightly confused, but rested. Restored. She rolls her shoulders, circles her head.

Liv smiles at Adam and only now notices that something's wrong. The story is finished, but he's not done yet.

No note of explanation, he whispers through clenched teeth. Not a sign of warning.

Liv gently squeezes Adam's arm. His muscles are tense; he's shaking.

152

Will you write this? he asks.

No, Liv says after a pause. Adam shakes off her hand.

Why not?! he shouts.

Liv points her stained fingertips towards Adam's face.

You know what this is? she asks. This is the price you pay for turning real stories into fiction.

She bends forward; picks up a couple of the pages from the ground. She passes them again to Adam.

Please take it, she says. Please?

Adam knocks the papers out of Liv's hand.

That's not good enough, he barks.

I'm sorry, Liv says. I really am. But that's all I have.

Not good enough! he screams.

Liv is about to turn away when Adam grabs her hand.

Let go, she says.

Adam stares at his own hand, clenched tightly around Liv's wrist. He seems surprised, as if he didn't plan it. But Liv notices that this unexpected demonstration of power pleases Adam; maybe it has even come as a revelation. The grip around her skin tightens.

Adam?! she says. You're hurting me, Liv tries to jerk her hand.

No, Adam says.

Let me go! she cries.

I will. If you write the story.

Adam pauses. Liv sees he hesitates before he decides to add: You either do what I tell you or you can't leave.

Liv pulls her hand as hard as she can; she manages to free herself. The redness of her skin quickly turns purple-blue.

Watch me, she says. She turns around; crosses the room. To make a step she must stamp on her writing; the pages cover every inch of the floor.

Liv, don't, she hears Adam's voice behind her. Please. Just write this story and everything will be fine... please don't walk out on me...

Liv halts. She's not to turn around again. From now on she's only to move forward, until she gets herself outside of the apartment, the building, the Estate. And so she barely looks over her shoulder. Still, she manages to see Adam, a cartoon character fuming with aimless rage.

Or what? she says. What is it you can do to me, Adam?

MARO

Liv's feet in trainers; that's what Maro sees first. He doesn't know why he doesn't just see her trainers. No, he specifically sees her feet, wrapped up in trainers as if in a bandage. As if they were injured.

He also doesn't know why he's been staring at the floor while opening the door. But now it seems impossible to take his eyes off the ground; off Liv's bandaged feet. And so he doesn't look up, doesn't say a word. He'd rather kneel, take off her shoes, see if she's hurt. But before he decides on his next step, a small painting falls on the floor, followed by an overcoat.

Maro bends to pick them up. His movements are earnest; the appearance of objects comes as a relief. With full hands he feels less exposed, more ready to face her.

I'll stay here tonight, Liv says. If that's ok with you?

Maro at last looks at her.

But Liv... he begins

Shush... she says. She puts her ink-stained finger on his lips.

Silenced, Maro doesn't dare to move either. Liv takes her finger away.

Your mouth! she grins. She bends forward and kisses him lightly.

When she pulls away, there is a blue stain of ink on her lips.

LIV

They lie with each other like a pair of snakes before shedding their skin. The sheets on the floor make for a lair; a hideout. Liv and Maro rub against each other's hard parts; jaws, elbows and knees. They bite the mouths, the nostrils, the ears. They hope to create a rupture, a rip. The pool water has loosened the old skin, the underground let them grow the new skin. When they wake up, they will leave the worn-out coating together with the dirty sheets. For they will wake up, they will sleep, Liv silently pleads. And when the night fades, she continues praying, they will crawl out of the den brand new.

How she found herself in Maro's apartment, Liv chooses not to remember. It is the Estate's right granted to its residents; to decline any responsibility for past actions. That's what this place is for; to let them walk out of their biographies, turn their backs onto the old selves. Behind the gate, behind the entrance door, they are allowed to immerse themselves into the underground. To bathe, to clean. To forget.

But it's a right, not a duty. And most of them have been adamant not to claim it. People without a future hesitate to abandon their past.

With no future and no past their present would've turned into an abyss; the world of the Estate is barren and discourages any form of life. And so some residents hold on to the memories the way infants look into mirrors; to confirm there's still a person behind their fragmentary experience. To reject the past is to lose oneself in the present that offers no boundaries, no horizons, no progressions. Their refusal to forget is a refusal to be forgotten.

That's also possible here; a life reduced to the past is yet another dimension that the Estate can nurture. The phantoms feed on the void; it's the perfect canvas. Their contours sharpen, their colours saturate. Soon the flatness of the image stops being enough. And so their past steps out, mighty and three-dimensional, gaining weight and gravity.

The world in which Maro has been living is an isolated place that admits no visitors. A world that Liv could never enter, never see what he sees. But tonight she's pulling him out to the other side, forcing him to use the privilege granted to the Estate's residents: a life with no past. A removal of the criminal record.

When they finally rest, they don't part. As if the tightness of their embrace leaves no space for anything but their bodies. If they let go, even just for a moment, the phantoms might slip in between, pushing them further apart. Liv's heel presses against Maro's ankle, his knee nestles in the back of hers. He's between her thighs, his armpits cover her shoulders. Their breaths synchronise.

Liv begins to fall asleep. Straight away she recognises the sensation; it's like riding a bike after a long break. It feels scary at first, but she's surprised to discover that her body still knows exactly what to do. But just as she is about to let go, about to fall, Maro sits up abruptly. His pulling away physically hurts Liv, as if someone removed a waxing strap from her skin.

She rolls around. Maro's body gleams in the dark, covered in sweat. He looks at her with wild, feverish eyes.

You shouldn't be here, he says.

Liv reaches out to Maro, gently stroking his arm.

Tell me a story, she says.

What story? he asks.

Helen's story, she says. What really happened, Maro?

She doesn't see it coming. One moment her hand moves across his perspiring skin, the other it's held captive in an iron clutch. Her head presses hard against the floor in an attempt to release the pressure from Maro's forearm, now weighing heavily on her neck.

His face is right above hers. She looks at it for answers, but then turns her eyes away with dread. His features are contorted, barely recognisable.

What are you talking about?! Maro shouts. His breath is so hot it feels like it could burn her skin, put fire to her brows and lashes. She forces herself to look at him again. The moment their eyes meet is like pressing the right button to prevent the explosion. Maro snaps out of his wrath; he rolls onto his back. But his hand remains clenched around her wrist. His grip is tight; just as tight as Adam's. But this time Liv decides not to break free. Even if he let her go, she couldn't leave just yet. Not before she knows whether she's been wrong all this time. Whether it's a different man she should've been afraid of.

Maro? What did you do to her? Liv says.

MARO

The skin on Liv's hand turns pale blue. He sees his grip like a dam; it impedes the flow of blood. For a moment this act of violence creates an illusion of power; a possibility. If he can block her circulation, he can also prevent the stream of memories from flooding his head.

Maro tightens the grip and holds for another few seconds. But the question that Liv asked has pierced a hole in the wall he built around the events; around Helen. The past is leaking through.

He can see Helen's face now, asleep on a deckchair.

Maro lets go of Liv's arm. Her skin is now bicolour; half dark beige, half pale blue. But Liv doesn't take her hand away; she holds it right in front of him. Maro's not sure what it is that she wants him to see; the hurt he has caused her or its impermanence.

For it is short-lived; fleeting. Soon the stream of blood, running freely again, will let the skin regain an even tone.

Even the bruise that already appears at the surface will last a couple of weeks at most. His aggression, like all violence, proved futile. It cannot stop the currents from running their course. Maro's powerless, defeated. The memories now drill a dozen holes, turning the wall into a sieve. The past pours through.

Helen's still asleep on a deckchair. A female hand nears her mouth and nostrils. It stops just an inch away from her face, as to avoid touching the skin. Helen breathes steadily.

Positive, says Anna. She's sleeping like a baby.

The group of nocturnals circle the deckchair in shock. Everybody's there: Thea, Titus, Sergei, Luca, Natasha and Alex. Not Maro though. He doesn't need proof; he already knows. And he cannot bear to see it.

What happened?! Sergei shouts.

Anna does not respond. She turns, looking behind the circle they form around her. She's searching for something, someone. But her permanently squinted eyes can't penetrate through the group, through the underground's dim light. She stands up, walks away from the nocturnals.

Now she knows he's watching them from a distance, he feels the cold of the wall against which he leans. He feels safe here, hidden in the shadow, untraceable. He watches Anna nuzzling around the underground; circling him without a trace of recognition. For a moment there he's certain she might've actually gone blind. But when she finally spots Maro, her eyes pierce through him like a pair of lasers.

What happened? She says out loud, so that the rest of the group hears and turns to them.

She fell in love, Anna then says.

LIV

Her arm begins to tremble. She tries to hold it still, as still as possible. The hand both burns and tingles. She wishes to circle the wrist, massage the aching skin. But it must remain in the same position until she forces Maro to speak. If she took it away, within a minute neither of them would've believed he had done it. Not someone like Maro; he's trained to assault himself, not others. But Liv knows that his outburst wasn't an attack; it was a reflex. As if she stuck her finger into his eye, or into a wound. He jerked, striking her in self-defence. And so now her stretched out, trembling arm is evidence not of his crime, but his injury. That's what she's after; the wound's narrative.

Why don't you ask Adam? Maro finally says. Just as his words spill, Liv's arm bounces back to her chest. She wraps the other hand around it and cradles it gently.

She watches Maro move to the verge of the lair. He sits up, turning his back to her. He refuses to talk; to answer her question. As if Helen's story wasn't his to tell. There seems to be a commemorative division in the Estate; each man mourns one of the women. Helen's story belongs to Adam, while Maro observes the memory of his late wife. Helen was erased from Maro's biography, whatever the two had shared. Just as Adam will never remember Liv as someone he lived with, no matter how long she had stayed with him in the Estate. His home belongs to only one woman; Helen.

Maro stands up and walks to the door. His silent withdrawal feels like an insult. She might have had a deal with Adam; she agreed to step in for Helen. She didn't just consent to being invisible; invisibility was her own demand.

But that deal never applied to Maro. Their relationship was based on sharing each other's secrets. They have become each other's intimates, even if it's not love that tied them together. What she accepted with Adam she cannot bear with Maro; she refuses to be obliterated from his biography.

I don't have to ask him! Liv shouts. Adam already told me.

Maro is right by the door, his hand lifted, about to grab

the handle. He halts; he must be hesitating. Liv knows that he'd like to leave without having to tell another thing; that he owes her no explanation. And that she made such silent retreat impossible. Her claim was a hook; even someone like Maro demands his right for defence. His hand drops, Maro turns around.

Told you what exactly? he asks.

About Helen, she says. And immediately feels ashamed. It's not that she lied; Adam did tell her what happened. It's that Liv didn't believe him. It's only Maro who can tell her this story.

But Maro says nothing; he watches her instead. Liv feels he's verifying whether she's telling the truth. As if just by looking at her he could tell whether she really knows. Would knowing what took place in the Estate before her arrival leave on her a palpable imprint?

He wanted me to write about her, Liv adds quietly.

And will you? he asks.

I don't collect stories, she says. I steal them, remember?

MARO

He now remembers that night in great detail. How his memory preserved an intact record of the events is a mystery. Maro hadn't thought about it once afterwards; not a scene or a word had been replayed again in his head. There were no nightmares, no regrets. If asked, Maro would've described the obliteration of Helen from his past as a mnemonic correction; none of this should've happened, none of it mattered. None then should have been remembered.

And yet here they are; the memories. An untouched footage of the night's events. It reminds Maro of the fresco paintings discovered on the walls of a little medieval chapel that he and Emily visited one summer, years before he moved into the Estate. For centuries the paintings remained hidden; wax from the candles which burned in the chapel coated the walls. The visitors lit candles for prayers; in the memory of people who were not there. But as the candles burned away and disappeared, it was the images on the wall, the images which no one paid attention to, that became immortalised.

Maybe the same thing has been happening to Maro; busy paying homage to his wife, he incidentally preserved Helen's story. And now it comes back to him, vivid and alive, transporting Maro into a night that should have never taken place.

He's on a deckchair, reading a book. The light is sharper than usual; it ruins the underground's intimacy, but makes it easy to read. And so Maro follows the change in the atmosphere dictated by the building and concentrates on the text. Then a splash of water rains over him; over the pages.

Maro looks up. Helen stands naked by the pool. The bright, clinical light makes her look older. But older than what? Maro's never asked about her age; never even bothered thinking about it. And yet the light makes her age apparent. It's not the freckled, porcelain skin; the skin that could coat a much younger body. It's something in her face; a threat that only bitterness is able to produce. It forces Maro to admit he was a fool believing he'd get away with this.

You can't make me leave! she cries. I love you, do you understand?

That's precisely why you've got to go, he says and turns back to his book. He turns it vertically; tries to shake off the water. But the drops had already soaked into the paper. Even when dry, the pages will be curled, the damage irreparable.

It's that love of yours that's to blame, Maro adds. He knows he should be quiet. But the displeasure at seeing his book ruined makes him want to hurt Helen; to whip her with words.

I'd have you stay, Maro continues without looking at her.

But that love you feel makes you sleep. And you know the rules. If you sleep, you don't belong here.

But I love you, Helen says.

You love me, yes, I know, he says. But what good is love that doesn't take away sorrow?

Helen roars in response. With a mane of red hair floating in fury around her head, she looks like a hurt lioness. There's something sublime about her rage; attractive even. But Maro's never liked cats; he's always been more of a dog person.

Helen takes a few steps back; she's now on the edge of the pool.

I'll drown myself! she warns.

No you won't, Maro says, his eyes fixed on the pages. You're not the type.

He knows Helen's exactly the type; she's stupid enough to kill herself in an attempt to hurt him. Even though she failed to make him feel a thing while alive, she probably believes that her death would force him to suffer the same loss that she's now experiencing.

How dare you?! she screams.

Really? Maro says.

You're a monster, she whispers.

Of course I'm a monster, Maro says, finally looking up. That's precisely what I am. It's a bit disappointing that it has taken you so long to notice.

Maro goes back to reading. He registers the sound; a splash of water. But he has other things to worry about; the wet pages stick together as if glued. It's nearly impossible to separate them without a tear.

LIV

Studying Maro feels like watching a silent movie. He stands still, but the expressions of his face, the micromovements of

162

his body, the energy with which he vibrates, make it impossible for Liv to take her eyes away. The footage is black-and-white. Literally; in the darkness of the night, amid the bareness of Maro's apartment, there are only two dimensions: the shade and the light. A couple of lamps outside the Estate illuminate the space through the translucent glass of the windows. The luminous streams create two bright islands. The lair on the floor belongs to Liv; she's the audience. The doorframe provides the contours for Maro's soundless performance.

Seeing Maro like this lets her learn more about him than the weeks that they spent talking. Something in him that always prevented Liv from seeing more than he was willing to disclose, is now gone. Maro seems to have forgotten about her; without moving an inch, he has been travelling far away from here. But that's not it. Often in the past Liv, unseen, would've tried stealing glances from a distance. And yet she could never catch him unguarded; to look behind the persona that he has created and mastered behind the walls of the Estate.

Liv knows that the current change in Maro has nothing to do with her; it's something he's now seeing. Wherever Maro's mind has arrived, it has made a discovery powerful enough to bring about a destruction; a turmoil. And Liv is forced to participate in it. She wishes she never looked inside Maro's shell, but it's too late now. There is a synchronicity to their discoveries; each of them is being made aware of Maro's crime in real time. And it resembles a matryoshka doll of corruption; behind each layer hides another one. The secret underneath is always darker than the one before.

The former crime, one that Maro has been carrying around like an open wound provoked Liv's fear, maybe even dread. But also pity. Maro, who never rested, was the greatest victim of his own wrongdoing. And a sole author of the wound's incurability; scratching it open to make sure it never heals. It was then no longer a crime, but a tragedy. True, getting to know his secret made Liv run away at first. But only for a short while. Ultimately, she's come back to him. Come back to save him.

But the crime they're uncovering now is different; it reveals Maro's most clandestine flaw. So well concealed that he had succeeded in dissociating himself from what he did; removing not just the responsibility for his actions, but the memory of what actually happened to Helen. That's how he succeeded in seamlessly hiding it from the world; he hid it from himself. There was nothing that could give him away, no evidence creeping out from underneath.

But that means it hits him unprepared; Liv can tell he never anticipated this moment would come. Never rehearsed the lies that could now fence him in.

Anyway, I already did, Liv says. It's an attempt to interrupt Maro's journey into the past; to take away the demand for a story that she's imposed on him. Maybe it's not too late, maybe they can still make it stop.

You wrote a story? Maro asks, returning back to her.

I did, Liv says.

Where is it?

Adam's apartment.

You left it with Adam?!

To Adam, Liv corrects him.

Like a deposit, Maro says.

More like a souvenir, Liv says.

You're not going back? he asks.

And I'm not staying here either, she says.

Maro pauses; he watches Liv very carefully. It seems as if he, too, was learning something new about her.

So why do you want me to tell you about Helen? he asks.

Maybe there is something you think I should know, she says.

MARO

Is there really something that either of them should know? Maro wonders. Liv would've had a right to know the truth, if it was the truth that she was after. If she was here to preserve Helen's story, Maro would've dug it out for her, no matter the costs. But he realises that she asks not about the past, but the present. She wants to know not about the woman who was here before, but about the man who stands right in front of her. And he made the mistake of believing it was a requirement for their life together. Now he understands that she's asked him to help her leave. The story is her way out.

So no, there is nothing that Liv should know, Maro thinks angrily. No matter what hides in the darkness of that night in the underground, she need not learn a single detail. You don't get to feed on others' secrets just so you can leave them. Dig in yourself, not in others, to find the strength.

But it also impresses Maro; that ability of Liv's to intuit exactly what she needs most in any given moment. He has seen her run the moment she sensed a threat. She wouldn't hesitate, wouldn't need a word of encouragement. But now it's different. Maro believes that Liv wants to leave the Estate without ever looking back. To do that, she must first satiate her curiosity; feel as if there isn't a crack she didn't look into. Like a brilliant child needing to understand the inner mechanism of every moving toy. Break them into pieces so she can look inside; cut them open.

A terrible, gritty shriek peals out. Maro shivers; looks down. Liv's hands press against the floor, her fingers curled, nails scratching against the wood. The sound they make emulates hundreds of tiny, nearly invisible splinters thrusting underneath the nails. Maro looks away from the floor, inhaling deeply to push away the sudden feeling of sickness.

His eyes land on Liv's body, follow its contours. She sits on the floor in a seemingly relaxed fashion, but Maro notices the tension that pulsates from her body. She might think it's the stress around the ominous discovery they're about to make. And maybe there's an element of thrill, like watching a scary film. But Maro knows Liv's tension indicates something else altogether; her readiness to take off. She lurks. The moment she catches a glimpse into the story of Helen's disappearance, she will jump. And with Maro's secret in her teeth, Liv will run away. A she-wolf.

But might there be something about Helen that he, Maro, should know? He can't answer this question without stepping back into that night, into the underground. Just a moment ago he'd decided not to do it; to press stop on the memory footage. He was going to leave it frozen exactly on the scene at which he had looked last; there was no need to look forward. But as Liv is about to run away from him, Maro knows he cannot run away too. He must stay, look himself in the face, no matter what he discovers. And so Maro steps back; ready to bear witness.

He finds himself still on the deckchair, reading. Or more accurately trying to read, as his fingers wrestle with the damp, fragile pages, eyes deciphering the smudged letters. It doesn't help that the light with every minute becomes dimmer. Maro feels as if he is racing against the Estate before it imposes a curfew and all the lights will be switched off.

There is something else that bothers him; makes it even harder to concentrate. The noise of repetitive splashes, as though something was fighting against the water.

And yet Maro doesn't look up; he's had enough of Helen's cheap manipulation. If you want to drown, just do it already and leave me in peace, he mumbles, gently turning the pages. But then the noise ceases, all at once. He should be glad, but the silence is all too sudden, too complete. Maro could swear it grows, expands, until the absence of sound becomes unbearable.

And so he looks up, turns to the pool. The water surface

is perfectly flat, still. On the side of the pool there is the silhouette of a man. Maro doesn't recognise him at first; at this point there is scarcely any light left in the underground. Maro puts down the book, sits up. He looks as hard as he can, against the lack of light. He can now see that the man kneels on the edge of the pool, his torso bent forward, his hands placed on the water. As if the pool's surface was solid and he was about to perform a series of press-ups.

Then Helen's head emerges between the man's arms, gasping for air. It lasts only a second or two. The man presses on her shoulders with apparent strength; she sinks right back down into the pool. Without a sign of struggle, like a piece of metal, or a rock. For sometime afterwards oxygen bubbles ruffle the water's surface. But after a while even they disappear.

Once again all Maro sees is the kneeling silhouette of the man. Of Adam, whom Maro now recognises without much surprise. Of a man just like Maro; a man who killed his wife.

LIV

She wishes that the lights outside would follow the example set earlier by the underground and grace them with pitch darkness. Liv imagines that it would fall on them like a heavy, velvet curtain at the end of a show.

But no; if anything the lights are even brighter, more unforgiving. They expose every crease of Maro's skin. Liv is aware it is the face of a man who has looked into the darkest place in the world; his own mind.

But she, Liv, has been there too. Not once has she taken her eyes off Maro during his journey. And she knows there isn't a crime in the world that now remains inconceivable to him; to them both. Not a human monstrosity that they can deny as something they would be incapable of. If you once deliberately injure the life of another, what guarantee can there be that you won't do it again, go a step further? For she's certain that is what Maro did; hurt Helen.

When earlier tonight Liv fantasised that their last time together would let them shed their old skins, she had imagined there was a brand new layer shining from underneath. But their old skins turned out to be a metal armour that prevented the growth of new cells; new life. Once they removed it, there was only the bare inside, uglier and more vulnerable than they would have let themselves believe. How wrong they have been all along, blaming themselves for tragedies they had no control over but denying responsibility for the crimes they authored. For whatever Maro had done to Helen, Liv, too, could have done it. Not to Helen, but to Adam. Or even to Maro; or anyone else she could have crashed into on the night she received the phone call.

But the point of no return from the people they wished they were becomes the place of their encounter. They look at each other. For the first time since they've met Maro's eyes are not just alert; they're alive.

I can tell you what happened to Helen, he says. Tell you what I've done.

Liv understands; he will not be running away from himself. She can see he's made up his mind. And so he becomes the only man in the world that she cannot run away from. They have incriminated each other; they have set each other free.

There's nothing to tell, she says.

But Liv… he begins.

There is nothing to tell, she repeats. Just come here, she whispers.

Maro hesitates, but then walks forward. He treads carefully, as if undeserving of every step that brings him closer to her. And so Liv stands up to meet him halfway. She takes his hand in her hand, leads them both back to their lair.

The night is not yet over. There is still time to lie down with each other; to sleep. Not as a pair of snakes, but two humans without skin.

8: MIKVAH

ADAM

It's a dark night. Neither the moon nor a single star competes with the Estate's lights. These are bright, surgical. But they are not here to let you see; they are to blind you. The windows of the apartments might be un-shuttered, but no one gets to look inside.

Adam stands in front of the building, breathing in the strange, acidic odour that the walls exude. He struggles to decode the notes; trace their source. It alarms him; he's used to recognising in a flash any given scent that he comes across. But it's as if his mind doesn't have a template to match the heady aroma that now saturates the air.

Maybe there is something wrong with him; maybe it's this story that Liv has left. It might've soaked into his skin, dulling the senses.

Adam looks down at the thick manuscript that he now presses against his chest with both hands. He came down here to dispose of it, just as he had thrown away everything that was left after Helen. It's the least he could do after being abandoned: regain control. Clean the space, wipe the surfaces.

Getting rid of Liv's manuscript should be easier than erasing the traces of Helen. He doesn't have to wait, doesn't need time to say goodbye. Even the rage he felt when Liv refused to grant his last wish was brief, like a thunder. It could've killed her then and there. But once the door closed behind her, all the strength had left Adam. He sat there, defeated, among the bastard pages that she inflicted on him.

How and when he began reading them, Adam cannot tell. All he knows is that he gulped them, page by page, until the last sentence. The story might have been a lie, but a lie that brought Helen back to him.

But the manuscript was also the only evidence of Liv ever being here; the only reminder of her refusal to stay. The thought again triggered his fury. Without thinking it through,

Adam decided to remove the pages from his apartment.

But once he's stepped outside, he realises he cares so little about Liv it wouldn't hurt him to keep her story. And if he read it often enough, he'd begin seeing it; experiencing the recounted events again and again. With time, it would no longer matter whether any of it happened in the world outside or inside his mind. The story would turn into a memory. When it comes to the past, it's always a matter of choice. Which of it to keep, which to erase. Why stick with facts that cause pain if you can choose a fantasy?

And so Adam makes up his mind; he's saving Liv's manuscript. Not as a reminder of her departure, but a parting gift. A souvenir.

The only thing that still bothers him is that heavy, alien odour that drapes the Estate. It distorts his perception of the place; makes it appear hostile. As if a lover showed up wearing an unrecognisable smell; the smell of someone else. As if he, Adam, was betrayed.

Unable to name the scent, he decides to break it down to a few familiar trails. He closes his eyes; the images first explode but then organise themselves in a mental, sensual mood board. An open freezer. A steaming, hard boiled egg. Fresh fish. Wet bark covered in moss. A web of mould spreading across the wall. And again; the steam, the icy air from the freezer, like a fishy, mouldy breath.

Adam opens his eyes. That's what it is. A breath; an ancient, night breath.

The building is awake; unlike its residents.

LIV

It's the middle of a summer day. The scorching heat makes the air taste like coarse sand, hurting the membrane of her throat and nostrils. Liv stands in front of the Estate. The windows to all the apartments are left wide open. To all but one; Robert's window is closed. He, too, now lives on the Estate. But Liv's not allowed to see him. They're not to meet ever again.

She takes her eyes off his apartment, looks down. But just as she's about to walk away, she remembers; he's not here. He's somewhere else, somewhere far. Taking a trip. Surfing.

And Liv knows straight away; she must walk into his home. See what's there; what Robert keeps inside.

The moment she steps into his apartment, she takes off her dress. It's not easy, the fabric sticks to her sweaty skin. It requires peeling off, inch after inch. When the dress at last falls down, she leaves it right there, at the doorstep, and walks to the bathroom.

Liv steps into the bathtub and turns on the shower. The stream of cool water washes off the sand, the sweat. Then something happens, like a glitch in a film. And Liv knows straight away; Robert's back. She turns off the water, rushes out of the shower. She grabs a small, white towel hanging on the wall. She dries herself in a hurry, then freezes just as rapidly. If Robert finds the wet towel, he will know. Liv was here; she broke into his home.

She puts the towel back, runs out of the apartment. Just as she flies out of the building, she sees Robert approaching the Estate. His head is down, eyes fixed on the ground. Liv understands that he is letting her get away with this. Grateful, she begins running in the opposite direction.

She runs fast, and for a long time. She gets out of the city, crosses fields and forests. Then her legs turn into hooves. She knows she cannot stop; she feels there is a chase after her. She decides to take random turns; to confuse the hunt.

And then she halts, surprising even herself. A thought paralyses her: no matter how far she runs, there is still the wet towel. Any attempt of escaping is hopeless; they will know she was there.

Liv sits up, gasping. She's back in Maro's apartment, but

the terror she feels belongs to the dream. It lingers with her for a few more seconds; she looks around the room to shake it off. Everything here appears exactly the same as when she had fallen asleep; when they had. Liv turns to Maro anxiously. He wriggles a little, as if even in his dreams he remains uncomfortable, letting himself rest. And yet here he is; sleeping. Liv chuckles, covering her mouth so as to not wake him.

She's about to lie down by his side, when she spots a darker shade in the corner of the room, like the contour of a person's silhouette. But she can't be sure; the outside lights that illuminate the apartment do not reach there. It's a blind spot. Liv leans forward, uncertain whether it isn't yet another dream. She squints her eyes to gain focus. Could it be…?

Adam! Liv shouts. But the sound never leaves her throat, never reverberates. It stops half way, suppressed by a tight hoop that closes around her neck. Pushed back inside, the cry explodes inside her. It presses against the skin that stretches out, swells, almost explodes. But as the hoop tightens, the cry quietens.

Adam steps out of the shadow into the cold, white light. It seems to freeze him; he stands completely still, with his eyes fixed on Liv. At first she doesn't understand what is happening. She can't speak, can't breathe. Where is Maro? And why is Adam just standing there, why won't he help release the suffocating hoop? It makes it impossible to breathe.

And then there is the glitch again. Like in movies. Like in her dream. And Liv understands. Maro was right; last dreams carry a message. She thought she could run away. But she forgot she left the wet towel.

MARO

A bang pulls him out from a chasm. That's where Maro's been in his sleep; he floated in nothingness. No dreams, no nightmares. A nocturnal limbo.

The moment Maro sits up, he shivers. A gust of icy wind lashes against his flushed skin. He looks to where the draught comes from. The fixed window is now open; it slams with force. That's where the noise has come from.

The windows in the Estate are never to open. Maro realises straight away; the building is back. Their falling asleep must have woken the Estate; goaded it into attack. Liv and he must prepare for trouble; Maro's never heard of anyone ever leaving the Estate alive. And he's one of the first to have moved here.

He quickly turns to Liv. She lies completely still, peaceful. As if she was in a place so distant that no sound could reach her.

She sleeps on her side; a bony shoulder sticks out from a veil of long hair that otherwise covers her face and her back. Maro leans forward; he kisses the island of her bare skin. The cold from Liv's body penetrates through Maro's lips, giving him chills. It's the wind; she must be freezing. Maro wants to grab the covers to tuck Liv in. But his hands struggle to grab the fabric; they're powerless, numb. As if he spent the night carrying heavy objects in his sleep.

He tries to regain command over his body, but another window opens; slams.

Liv doesn't even jerk. Sleep seems to have turned her into a stone; cold and motionless. But that's how it should be; she needs all that time to make a recovery. Still, he should hurry before yet another bang succeeds in waking her up.

Maro tries to get up quickly but his legs are as stiff as his hands, as if sleeping has sapped all his strength.

When he finally manages to stand up, the last window

opens. Now all of them close and open in turns. Each time they open faster than before, slam with a greater force. As if the building was screaming; the nearer he comes to the windows, the louder it yells.

Maro tries to seize the windows, but then realises that fixed frames don't have handles that he can lock. All he can do is to wait out the storm.

Maro heads back to Liv, accompanied by the escalating noise. If they lived anywhere else, the neighbours would've been storming his doors, furious to be woken up. But here nobody sleeps.

Maro halts, stricken with dread. In a flash he grasps what has happened here tonight; what he's done. But he closes his eyes, about to pray: Let it not be true. Then he remembers; he's used up all his credit. There are no more prayers left.

He looks straight ahead, at whatever is left of Liv. He stretches out his hands, at once recognising the cause of their frailty upon waking. Slaughter.

He fights off the impulse to rush to her, to lift her up, press against his chest. He will not let himself to ever touch her again. Then for another moment he wishes to collapse his legs, to close his eyes, weep.

But he gathers all the self-discipline he's trained in over the years and forces himself to remain still. He sums up the courage she's given him to look straight into his last crime.

Maro stands guard, while the windows continue raging.

The longer he stands there, the more he hears that the scream expresses not hostility, but despair. It's not even a scream, but a lamentation. The building is crying.

ADAM

At the crack of dawn the underground is empty and undisturbed. It smells of its usual mixture; cigarette smoke and bodily fluids. There is also the smell of death, but Adam's sure no one could detect it but him.

Just a moment ago the lights came back on. Now the dim, warm glow once again illuminates the walls. As if nothing ever happened here.

At first glance everything looks the same as when Adam was here last. He knows exactly when it was: the night when Helen left. Not how long ago though; he doesn't mark the passage of time the way others do. There are days and there are nights; he doesn't need to know how many. What he cares about are eras; before and after the Estate. Before and after Helen.

But tonight Helen's fading away. It's a night of purge, the night of mikvah. And so Adam's stepped back into the underground to immerse himself in water; to wash himself clean. Whatever period will commence tomorrow, he wanted to be ready.

But he was wrong to believe this was the end; wrong to declare new beginnings before the night was complete, before he'd had a chance to see it through.

It has been so long since Adam had heard the splash of water. It was the promise to cleanse that lured him in. He couldn't know that the underground ceased offering redemption. That it has become a trap instead. That he would be snared.

Now he finds himself in yet another corner, unsure whether he's seen enough tonight, whether he'll be let go. From where he stands, only half of the pool is visible. The deckchairs next to it are empty. Right behind them is the entrance. All he needs to do is get to the pool, clean the last night's mess, and then get to that door, unnoticed. Maybe he can still save the underground, save the Estate.

But just as he moves forward, a distinct whiff of heavy detergents and synthetic floral airspray hits him in the face. All of it mixed up with fresh, human sweat. Immediately after follows the sound of approaching footsteps and another sound. Like wheels rolling across the floor. Adam pulls back, pressing as hard as he can against the wall.

He watches from his hideout how the door opens; very slowly, as though with effort. A large cleaning trolley slides through the door. The main lights switch on, bright and crisp. Behind the trolley is a heavy, middle-aged woman dressed in a uniform jacket, sweatpants and cheap trainers. Adam remembers he's seen her around the Estate whenever he has to rush to work early. She must be one of the Estate's invisible housekeepers.

Adam notices that aside from the rubber gloves, the woman wears headphones. He relaxes and exhales loudly; at least he doesn't need to keep quiet. Loud disco comes through the woman's headphones; there is not a chance she could hear him.

The woman pushes the trolley further inside. She parks the trolley, grabs a large bin bag and walks towards the deckchairs and side tables.

The bright light reveals the mess at the side of the pool. There are used towels, empty beer cans, empty wine bottles, cigarette butts; a post-party scene. She begins picking up the rubbish, her back to the pool. She hums incomprehensibly, a foreign song. It's the right place for it; they are all foreigners here.

The woman stops; she half-turns, as if she spotted something on the floor, close to the pool. She walks a few steps and crouches with her back to Adam, facing the pool.

The beat from his heart muffles the beat vibrating from the woman's headphones; it's louder.

She picks up a used condom from the floor and sighs with disdain, shaking her head in a gesture of disbelief.

For a split second Adam truly believes that the condom might be the only thing she spots this morning. Gratified with the minor discovery that confirms her opinion about the

Estate's transgression, she will turn away, quickly wrapping up the rest of her duties. She would leave then, letting Adam handle the rest of cleaning. Even though it's not his mess.

But then the woman halts. Adam only sees her profile, but he knows straight away what it is she's staring at. It takes her a while to take it in; to comprehend. But once she gives herself permission to recognise the horror she stumbled upon, the woman's mouth lets out a terrible scream.

Adam shivers. He doesn't mind the sound, but feels revolted by the smell of an early morning breath, the half-digested bacon roll.

He steps out from the corner, and walks past the screaming woman. He's certain that the shock she's now experiencing makes his escape safe; to leave unnoticed. Just before he exits, Adam glances over his shoulder at the pool.

Maro's naked body is floating in the water.

Adam sighs with resignation; nothing here will ever be quite the same.

SHE WAS NEVER HERE

ALICE

Adam's hands have the softest skin Alice has ever touched. It's as if he was walking around in invisible gloves; nothing he comes in contact with leaves a mark on him.

Not that Alice ever really got to feel his hands; not the way she would've wanted. Just a few seconds here and there, stolen under the pretext of cordiality or support. But all she really needed was a single instance of their skins meeting each other to create a memory more powerful than if it were built of images or words.

She now watches Adam close his hands into fists and slowly, as though with effort, open them up again. Earlier this morning he surprised her by offering a hug instead of the usual handshake. She hid her disappointment in his shirt, pressing her cheek against its cotton, pretending the fabric wasn't there. Instead, she imagined that her face sank into his chest hair. The shirt felt damp, as if Adam spent the night running in rain. Or in a marathon, Alice wouldn't be able to tell the difference between rain or sweat. Wet is wet; it feels exactly the same.

She forces herself to take her eyes off Adam's hands; he hasn't invited her here to contemplate his physique. No; he needs her help. The woman's gone again; this time for good. Just as Alice predicted.

They sit together on the sofa; the only piece of furniture in Adam's living room. That's another thing she loves about him; the consistency. Adam's apartment looks just like his office, just like his desk. Ascetic, sleek. Just like Adam himself.

And you're sure she didn't take anything with her? Alice asks.

I told you already, Adam says. She took nothing.

Fine, she says. But did she maybe leave something?

Adam jumps up. It looks like an involuntary reaction, the way a leg kicks out when a doctor hits a spot just below the knee cap. He crosses the room; halts once the distance between them makes it impossible for Alice to track the expressions on his face.

Like what? he snaps. What would she leave?

I don't know... Alice says, surprised with the hostility in his voice. People don't just disappear without a trace. They always leave something. A pair of earrings, a notebook... something.

A strange, muffled sound carries through the walls. Alice tunes into it. The sound gets louder; she's almost certain it's a cry of approaching sirens. Either police or ambulance, it's hard to tell. Maybe both.

She stayed here with you for a while, Alice continues after a pause.

Yes, and she used my things, Adam says. Even the clothes she wore were mine. She had nothing with her when we met. Just a pair of sneakers and a trench coat.

Okay...Alice nods. So she didn't bring or take anything....

She scans the room, ready to test the validity of this claim. But the moment she begins walking around, she realises that the idea is absurd. There are no shelves to investigate, no closets that would hide secrets, no tables underneath which she could now look. There's only the bare floor; bare walls.

Alice catches herself thinking: that's how Liv must've walked around here when she first moved in with Adam. In disbelief of finding herself in a place that bears no signs of life.

Adam stands at some distance; she feels his eyes on her, following her every step. Alice glances over him briefly, then resumes her tour. She presses her hand flat against the wall and begins to move it slowly, trying to get a sense of this place.

So strange... she says as though to herself. It's like she was never here.

Just as she finishes the sentence, her fingertips come

across a crack in the wall. Alice closes her eyes and lets her
hands guide her. The fissure is wide but very shallow. Not a
hole really, more a scar after a failed attempt to drill one.

She opens her eyes and turns to Adam

What's that?! she asks, trying to contain her excitement.

Adam's face is still too far away to reveal what he's
thinking. She can only rely on his words; his answer. But
before Adam gets to respond, the cry of sirens reaches the
apartment and reverberates full volume, making it
impossible to focus on anything else.

Alice runs to the window.

Oh God, you must see this! she exclaims, looking outside.
There's a mini army of police in front of your building.

ADAM

Alice sits with the police officer on the sofa; they're looking
at photographs of Liv's dead body.

Luckily, there isn't enough space for a third person. Adam
stands behind them, pretending he's joining in. But his eyes
are closed. No one should blame him; Adam saw enough last
night.

All he needs now is to relax; rest. The police visit is
almost over. And it's nothing but a formality; he knew even
before the officer entered the apartment. When the doorbell
rang, a whiff of bodily odour travelled across the corridor
and reached the living room, at once bringing Adam a sense
of relief. It was gentle, peaceful even. Like a fragrance that
little children have; warm and powdery. Few adults get to
smell like this; you have to sleep at least ten hours a night
and take regular, long naps throughout the day. This way the
dreams superimpose themselves onto the waking reality,
ensuring you never grow up. Adam's confident that such a
bodily odour has never before been detected in the Estate.

How anyone could endure such a smell while working on

a criminal investigation, Adam couldn't tell. Maybe the job remained part of a childhood fantasy about fighting evil forces? Adam didn't know; didn't care. All that mattered was the information decoded in the sweet, creamy notes; Adam was to be informed, not interrogated. The police ringing his door wanted to bring comfort, consolation. There were no reasons for further stress or worry.

Wait….he really just choked her? Adam hears Alice ask. While they were both asleep?

There is no evidence of fighting, the officer says. She might not even have woken up.

She did wake up, Adam wants to say. She woke up and looked straight at me. She might not have fought, true. But she begged me for help. Silently, with her eyes. And I would have helped her. I just really couldn't help him.

Oh, Adam! Alice exclaims.

He quickly opens his eyes. He's flustered, panicky. These were just thoughts, Adam tries to calm himself down. He didn't say any of this out loud; they can't read his mind.

He looks at Alice anxiously. She has turned around to face him; dangles the gruesome photographs of Liv in front of his face. Adam glances at them, then abruptly looks away.

Take this away! he screams.

It comes as a surprise, as much to Alice and the officer, as to Adam. The night must've shaken him up more than he has previously assumed. He must stay alert; watch out for every step and gesture. The officer might be an aged kid, but kids often get the sharpest instinct.

Adam collects himself, shoots them an apologetic look.

I'm sorry... he says. I just really cannot look at her… like this. It's too painful.

That's absolutely fine, the man responds. We've got all we needed. The family already identified the body.

Alice puts the photographs away on the table. She then gently squeezes Adam's hand. She lingers far too long, but

Adam lets her. He needs her on his side.

We don't have any questions, the officer continues. Unless there is something you think we should know.

Alice looks to Adam with a question. Is there? her face seems to say. But Adam just turns to the officer and shakes his head.

Well, then the case looks pretty straightforward to me. Mr Solice suffered from a condition known as night terror, 'pavor nocturnus'. It led to a tragedy previously in Mr Solice's life. Years ago he killed his wife in his sleep, in nearly identical circumstances. We have no reasons to believe it was anything else in this case.

But this time he couldn't bear it. And so he killed himself... Alice mumbles.

Well, yes, the officer admits. Suicide is our strongest hypothesis. The investigation will of course give us more certainty.

Alice bends forward and picks up the photographs. She scans through them frantically. Each photograph, once seen, lands on the floor. When there are no more photographs left in Alice's hands, she runs out of the room, covering her mouth.

Adam watches her with surprise; he's always believed Alice not to have a delicate bone in her body.

ALICE

The matter from her stomach is like a wild-fire that burns everything it meets on its way. She wishes she'd had breakfast before she headed out here; something solid that she could now throw up, instead of squeezing the juices out of her gut. But maybe that's exactly what should be pouring out of her on a morning when two people have just been slaughtered; a yellow acid. Maybe it's necessary to make her feel the burn of this loss.

She embraces the toilet with both her arms, soaking in the cold of the porcelain through her skin. It cools her down, brings relief.

When the nausea subsides, Alice pulls away from the toilet to stretch out on the floor. She lets her body calm down; to absorb the cool, rugged texture of the tiles. She lies flat, moving her head to the sides, rubbing each cheek against the floor.

After a while she sits up, ready to head back to the living room, back to Adam. But just as she is about to stand she notices a pile of papers stuck behind the toilet. She bends forward and pulls them out.

The pages are handwritten, and Alice can tell straight away that it's not Adam's writing. She runs her fingers against the ink letters; the touch sends chills down her spine.

It's Liv's new book, Alice can sense it. A book she will never finish.

There is a knock on the door.

Everything all right there? Adam asks through the door.

Alice looks at the manuscript in panic; does Adam know it's here?

Another knock on the door.

Alice? Adam repeats.

I'll be right there! she shouts.

She flips through the pages, desperately hoping to find something that could help her make up her mind. Straight away she notices that nearly every page contains the same word, 'Helen'.

You were writing about Helen! Alice whispers, excited. Her first impulse is to run outside; share her discovery. But then she remembers that Liv's previous book led to her partner's suicide. And she cannot allow anything to happen to Adam. She must protect him.

There is only one solution; she must stay here and read the manuscript. If it's in any way defamatory to Adam, she will destroy it without ever telling him she found it.

Alice?! Adam shouts through the door. What's going on there?

I'm sick! she shouts back, hoping it will buy her time.

ADAM

Nearly an hour after the door has closed after the officer, Alice reappears in the living room. Her usual odour is masked by an unusual mixture of vomit and adrenaline.

You never told me you write... Alice says.

Adam stares at her with confusion.

Write? He asks. Write what?

That manuscript? In the bathroom?

If there was a heavy object around, he would've smashed it against her head without giving it as much as a thought. But the space is entirely empty and he lacks Maro's strength to use his bare hands as a weapon. He considers the kitchen knives, but by the time he makes a step towards the kitchen, a new idea emerges.

Ah that, he says with a dismissive shrug. How embarrassing. You know, after Helen left, I had no one to talk to... and so, you know, got to get it out somehow.

It's good stuff, Adam. You should show it to someone.

Don't be silly, he says. It's pure nonsense.

Adam walks up to Alice. He takes her face in his hands; gently runs his palm across her mouth, nostrils. Alice begins to tremble.

Why are you looking at me like this?

Like what? He asks.

I don't know, she says. You're scaring me...

Adam hesitates. He then unexpectedly kisses her.

Am I still scaring you?

10: RACOONS

16: Raccoons

ALICE

Adam's breath tickles Alice's neck; he's trying to look over her shoulder. She has almost finished the book; she's reading the last page, last lines. She presses her finger against the page, moving along each word that she reads. It gives her a different sense of the story than when she read the handwritten pages. The manuscript she found might have belonged to Liv, but this printed book is Adam's, and Adam's alone.

Incredible, Alice sighs. She moves her eyes from the book onto Adam, who lies by her side.

It's still quite new to her; to have that infinity of his skin within arm's reach.

You think? Adam murmurs, leaning towards her.

He does it a lot now; comes near her. He lets her revel in the proximities of their bodies, the warmth that radiates from his skin.

Alice hits Adam with the book; it's her attempt to be playful.

I think?! she exclaims. It's a masterpiece!

Alice closes the book; weighs the hardback with a sense of awe. She turns it around to the front cover and reads with ceremony: Adam Spence, *The Objects She Left Behind.*

She notices that Adam still winces hearing those words said out loud. It's a grimace of dread, but Alice thinks that from the outside it could look like humility.

She tests it, ruffling his hair with tenderness, as if endeared by his display of modesty.

He lets her; they're safe.

ADAM

Alice has been asleep for one hour and forty seven minutes. For one hour and forty seven minutes Adam has kept his eyes closed. Their relationship has altered his perception of time;

he has become relentless in keeping count of it. It helps him pull through.

Every night Adam pretends to be asleep in case Alice wakes up; she wouldn't have understood. But then he lies there for a while longer, imagining he's dreaming. And that's not for her; it's for himself.

He now gets up, exits the bedroom, leaves the apartment. He walks through the corridors, fighting off the incessant feeling of confusion.

Alice's moving into the Estate didn't just take away his sleep; it dulled his sense of scent. At first it didn't feel like a loss, not quite. Unable to smell anything, Adam has gained an endless capacity to share a life with Alice. Had he still been able to detect every note of her odour, it would be only a few days before he, too, would end up floating dead in the pool. But straight away he was granted a way out; the moment he pressed his mouth against Alice's and pushed his tongue inside it, he could no longer smell a thing.

Now there is something that the two of them have in common; they share the same obscure condition, anosmia.

There are days when Adam sees his sudden loss of scent as a mode of self-preservation; proof of an inexhaustible adaptability of the human body, its willingness to survive no matter what. If you can't remove the source of stench, you stop smelling it all together.

But deep inside, Adam knows that it has little to do with Alice; it's between him and the Estate. He has been disarmed, made dependable.

Supposedly, anosmia only takes away your sense of smell. But the real consequences run deeper; you lose control. Every space you find yourself in is like a minefield; there is no way of telling which of your steps might cause an explosion. And as you lose control over yourself, your environment gains control over you.

Adam then wanders around the Estate like an old dog;

suspicious, disoriented. With both hands on the walls to balance his every step, he reaches the underground. The lights are off; Adam uses the torch in his phone to make his way. He reaches the sign 'No entrance' that has been placed here ever since the murders; trespasses it.

He walks all the way to the edge of the pool. He halts there, using the torch to illuminate the pools inside. At the bottom of the now empty bowl, there are the 'nocturnals': Luca, Sergei, Natasha, Anna, Thea and Titus.

Adam pauses, taking in the view of his tribe; his people. They are emaciated, drained; each of them a ghost of their former self. The light blinds them, causing a moment of confusion. But once they recognise it's Adam, they all jump towards him hungrily.

Have you brought the book?! Sergei shouts.

Have you? Natasha repeats.

Oh, just read it already! Thea rushes him, pulling the leg of his trousers.

Adam lifts up the book; Liv's book. The book she has given him. The only object she left behind.

The pool tingles with excitement.

Adam jumps inside. He sits at the bottom of the pool, surrounded by the hungry audience. He opens the book but takes a moment longer before he begins reading. He wants all of them to gather around; get ready.

Once they all believed they were young lions and lionesses, Adam finally begins, directing the torch to the pages. Nomadic and nocturnal. They did not know just yet that there were boundaries to their wandering.

Adam pauses, putting down the torch. One by one, he looks at each of the ruined faces. Their eyes shine bright enough to let him see their features, their tension. They listen with greed, careful not to miss a single word.

They still don't know that the time and place transformed them into racoons, living off urban waste and road kill,

Adam tries to continue. But the reading is interrupted by a muffled noise that comes from outside the pool. Ever since Adam lost the sense of scent, his hearing seems to have improved. He now pauses, alarmed.

The nocturnals all look towards the entrance, tuning in.

There is a distinct sound of approaching footsteps, and then the door opens.

The nocturnals all jump down to the floor. They lay flat on their bellies, with their eyes shut. As if they could compress, make themselves disappear.

Adam doesn't join them. Instead, he walks up to the edge of the pool; looks out. A stream of light from the corridor reveals the presence of a young man, standing in the doorstep. He looks hesitant, as if pondering something. After a moment the man makes a few steps into the darkness.

But right then, there is a sound of someone else running behind him.

Andy? a woman's voice asks.

The man pauses, letting the woman catch up with him. She wears a nightgown; looks both distressed and ruffled, as if she has just woken up.

Andy! she repeats, grabbing the man's arm. What are you doing here?

The man stares at her. Adam knows this look all too well; it's how Helen and Liv used to look at him. How he must be now looking at Alice. As though he struggles to recognise who she is and what she might want from him.

Huh? he says, confused.

Why are you here? the woman asks.

Just couldn't sleep, he shrugs, as if he was trying to get rid of a fly.

And you came here? Why? The woman continues probing. I told you the pool has been shut ever since that tragedy.

The man does not respond. She steps closer and takes his

hand.

Let's go back, she pleads. I don't really like being here at this hour of the night.

You go, Andy says, letting go of her hand.

Taken aback by his refusal, the woman remains still. She looks as if she is about to cry. The man turns to her; smiles gently.

I'll be right there with you, he says. I promise.

The woman stands a few seconds longer, then leaves. The man turns back to the pool; steps forward.

Acknowledgments

I would like to extend my sincere thanks to all the kind strangers who generously provided me with time and space so that I could find my voice in a foreign language and tell my story:

Alex Meurice (Slate Projects)

Nuoren Voiman Liitto (Villa Sarkia Residence)

Nina Rodin (Trelex Residency)

I am also grateful to my dearest friends and first readers, Georgina Parfitt, Emily Collett and Agi Bezeczky, for their invaluable suggestions and guidance.

Special thanks to my international tribe who relentlessly supported and nurtured me: Sake, Aga, Jeanne, Jordan, Julia, Josi, Mila, Matilda, Alina, Sean, Joanna, Ruth &Avi, Loyse & Ale, Krzysztof, Andrzej, Charlotte, Calum, Claudia, Ali, Sagrado, Yael, Isis and Henry.